Matters of Life and Death

Matters of Life and Death

Philip M Stuckey

Bridge House

British Library Cataloguing in Publication Data
A Record of this Publication is available from the British Library

ISBN 978-1-907335-85-3

This edition published 2020 by Bridge House Publishing
Manchester, England

Cover illustration © Jim Donnelly (Anaxa Images)

Contents

Witch in a Bottle

'In your own time, sir, and please, stick to the facts.'

'The facts?'

I am required to provide a statement for the young police officer who sits before me now, poised with notepad and pencil in hand. But how am I to account for events I cannot begin to understand? And yet, account for them I must, and then make peace with God. But as to the *facts* of this matter, I am no more reliable than the village cat.

'Yes, Reverend, we are here to establish facts. We are not interested in conjecture, embellishments or justifications... so when you're ready, please begin.'

It is the grim-faced inspector standing at the constable's side who addresses me now. The weariness of his tone suggests that he is simply going through the motions. I believe this man has already made up his mind.

'Very well, Inspector, I will relate, as far as I am able, the circumstances that have brought me here in ruins. But as to whether this information constitutes fact, I cannot be certain.'

I take a deep breath and begin...

'...It was the farm labourer, Jack Higgins, who brought it to me that fateful night, rousing me from slumber with his great fists upon my door. He looked like a ghost in the wan, yellow glow of my oil lamp, but I could see something in his hand that glistened like a cat's eye.

'I asked Jack what brought him there at such an ungodly hour, and he held out his glistening prize as though it were an offering.

'I adjusted the light so I could get a better look at the thing. It appeared to be a small, silver bottle, sealed with wax. I was irritated at having my sleep disturbed by what appeared to be a trivial matter and asked him if it couldn't have waited until morning.

6

'He placed both the bottle and a small scrap of parchment into my hand, stating emphatically, "No, Reverend, it could not," and before I could engage him further, he turned and fled into the night.

'Feeling confused but also intrigued by this strange and unexpected event, I closed the door and took Jack's bottle to my study, where I placed it upon my desk along with the parchment. I could see now that the bottle was of an unusual design, consisting of two bulbs, one larger at the base and one smaller at the top, separated by an elegant narrow waist. The contents of the bottle were obscured by a silvered lining of some kind and the top was sealed with wax, just as I'd thought.'

'And where is this bottle now?' the inspector interjects, disturbing my train of thought.

'I do not know, Inspector,' I lie, without conscience.

'I see. You mentioned parchment?'

'Yes. I then turned my attention to the parchment, noticing that there were words upon it. Turning up the light, I examined the writing through my magnifying lens and was shocked at what I read.'

I paused then, regathering my thoughts before continuing, determined to relate every nuance to the officers in the vain hope they would come to understand.

'Go on, Reverend. The words were?'

I swallowed hard, remembering…

'Here be the remains of Agnes Simpson, Witch. Open at thy peril.

'Despite my curiosity, I resolved to wait until morning to investigate the thing further and returned to my bed, where my sleep was filled with strange, lucid dreams and the new day brought me down to breakfast agitated and far from rested.

'My housekeeper, Mrs Barrowman, had prepared my boiled eggs and tea as always, but had departed without a word, adding to my sense of unease. I determined there may be something unusual stirring my flock and I resolved to find out what it was. How had Jack come to be in possession of such a curious artefact and what had made him appear so afraid?'

'I assume it is usual for people to come to you with matters that are of concern to them, Reverend?'

'As you are aware, Inspector, the village of Little Pemberton nestles in a fold between two hills, where the infant stream has not yet become the adolescent river. The road in is a difficult one, so few ever come and go, save the fifty or so souls that reside there, scattered amongst smallholdings, cottages and shepherds' huts. Farm workers they are, in the main, hardy, simple folk and dependable. They built the chapel with their own hands and fill it every Sunday without fail. I have come to know them as my own family these past ten years. The Landowners are the Wright family from nearby Longridge, but they are often absent. It is left to me to care for the well-being of this small community and they have accepted me well enough into their midst.'

The young officer raises his eyebrows at this, and I can't blame him for I speak as though nothing has happened. But he cannot know what is in my heart. The inspector is experienced and shows little emotion, already convinced of my madness.

'Indeed, please do continue, Reverend. And I wish to know every conversation you can remember in as much detail as possible.'

'Very well, Inspector.'

I close my eyes and replay the memories of the previous days, reliving them in all their horror. I relate my tale as though it were a fiction and not simply a retelling of my own fate. With a shudder, I continue…

8

'After breakfast I returned my attention to the bottle and the strange note that accompanied it. I am not a superstitious man, or at least I did not consider myself to be so, but I knew something of what must have befallen Agnes Simpson if her remains were indeed contained within. Although it is true that women are no longer persecuted as witches, burned or hanged on flimsy evidence construed to be the work of the Devil, there are still places, remote and insular places, places like Little Pemberton, where the old fears still linger.

'I placed the bottle into the pocket of my coat and went out to greet the day. The sky hung low upon the hills, threatening rain. I pulled up my collar, put on my hat and followed the lane that led down and across the upper fields towards Jessop's farm. It was as I approached the standing stone at Withen Point the attack came. I registered the dark shape from the corner of my eye as it swept down upon me, but too late. It was a bird, a raven, and intent on doing me harm. Though I raised my arms in defence, my reactions were slow and the creature broke through, drawing blood from my scalp. I staggered forward, dazed by the impact, and the dark menace came at me again. Fortunately, my hand found a rock and I was able to fend off this second assault without taking further damage. The bird wheeled away with a shriek, leaving me reeling.

'I kept going, and as I approached Jessop's farm I could see the man himself, mending a fence at the perimeter of the lower field, with his dog in attendance. He must have sensed something was wrong because he threw down his tools and came striding towards me.

' "Reverend Greenacre, whatever has befallen you this mornin'?"

' "An encounter with an angry raven, John," I replied.

'We met at the gate and he checked my injured head.

9

' "That's a nasty one," he said. "Better let the missus clean that up."

' "Very well," I replied. "Thank you. I was hoping to discuss something with you anyway."

'We sat around his kitchen table staring at the bottle as Mrs Jessop cleaned and dressed my wound. There was an awkward silence that I took to be their great discomfort at seeing it.

'I asked John if he knew how Jack Higgins came by it. He replied that he did not.

' "I would like to speak with him about it. Do you know where I will find him today?"

' "Well, I didn't see him at the inn last night, which is unusual for Jack. Sometimes he chops logs for Alec Mortimer, over at Sherriff Wood."

' "That's a fair trek across the moor. I will visit the Hall on the way. Maybe the Wrights will know something about it."

' "Something don't feel right about that thing, Reverend," remarked Mrs Jessop. "I would bury it if I were you... or throw it down the old mine."

' "Thank you, Mary, but it has pricked my curiosity," I said. "I will discover its heritage if I can and dispose of it then. It may be of some interest to a city museum."

'I noticed the furtive glances between husband and wife but chose not to press them further. I decided it was time to leave.

'I thanked John for his care and for his hospitality, and asked him if he would see me on my way.

'We were back to the farm gate before John spoke again.

' "Take care, Reverend," he said at last. "There's history to this place that not everyone knows about."

' "Indeed so, but I'm not a man prone to superstition.

This artefact is of historical and maybe scientific interest, but that is all."

'At that I took my leave and made my way towards the ridge at Highcliffe so that I could get to the Hall by the shortest route. I had no idea if there would be anyone there to greet me, but it was worth a try. Reverend Charles Wright was of another parish, and retired, but would surely understand my concern.

'The Jacobean Hall graced the horizon as I dropped down past the brook at Hollow Crag. It is an impressive sight and one of long standing, built soon after the plague brought this place to its knees in 1665. I pondered that sorrow as I made my way through the gardens to the imposing front entrance. I announced my presence with a peal of the doorbell and was soon greeted by the friendly face of Alice, the maid.

' "Good day to you, Reverend Greenacre," she said, with a warm smile.

' "And the same to you, Alice. Might the Reverend be accepting callers today?"

' "I'm sure he will be for you, sir. Would you care to step inside?"

'The entrance hall was beamed and oak-panelled, rather like the chapel, but with a greater sense of grandeur. Family portraits hung on the walls next to tapestries and plaques of various descriptions. I felt diminished somehow by the sight of it.

'Alice had gone to fetch the Reverend and soon after, he appeared, dressed all in black as is his preference. He's a tall and slim man with a stern, grey face that now regarded me dispassionately.

' "This is a most unexpected pleasure," he announced, without sincerity. "How may I be of service to you, Reverend?"

' "It is a curious and perhaps sensitive matter, Reverend Wright. May we retire to your study?"

'He ushered me through the oak door to the right of the hallway and into a small library. I'd been here once before but not for some time. We sat on leather reading chairs, beside a grand fireplace, the fire now cold in the grate. It was a room I could certainly take pleasure in, surrounded by books of all types and art of great worth.

' "Tea?" he asked, cordially, but I was not there on a social visit.

' "No thank you, Reverend, this shouldn't take long."

'I brought out the bottle from my pocket, along with the scrap of parchment and passed both to him across the card table which separated us. He took them from me with trembling hands. His face had drained of what little colour it had and for a moment he could not speak. I noticed him swallow hard.

' "Where did you discover such a thing?" he asked.

' "Do you recognise it?" I watched his eyes.

' "No. No I do not," he said, "but it is a strange thing is it not?"

'I felt certain this was an untruth, which in itself was extraordinary, but I chose not to challenge him.

' "What about the name on the parchment?" I asked.

'He put on his reading spectacles and brought the parchment near to his face, accentuating further the nervousness he clearly felt.

' "Agnes Simpson," he muttered. "No, I've never heard the name."

'Another lie.

' "Might you have access to historical records that could shine some light on the name?" I probed.

' "What about your own church records?" he countered.

' "Only recent entries are registered and recorded," I said, knowing that he understood this already. "The

12

majority are held at Longridge. I could write, I suppose. But I'm sure your own land and tenant records go back as far as the great plague and beyond, do they not?"

' "Perhaps," he said, regaining some of his composure, "but the archives are locked away in storage. It would take a great effort, and I'm not sure it is worth it."

' "Very well, Longridge it is then." I stood, indicating that our conversation had reached its conclusion. "Thank you for your time, Reverend Wright."

'I returned the bottle and parchment to my pocket and made to leave, but he placed his hand upon my arm.

' "Do not pursue this further, Thomas," he said. "The past is best left alone. Who knows what frightful truths may be uncovered and what trouble it may cause if we choose to rake over the past. Leave the bottle with me and I will dispose of it."

' "Whatever do you mean, Charles?" I asked. "The past is dead and gone. All that remains are curiosities such as this. At least I must find out where Jack discovered it."

'Mention of the name raised his eyebrows.

' "Jack? Jack Higgins?" he asked.

' "Yes, the same," I replied.

' "Throw it into the old mine," he said then, with a dismissive gesture of his hand, "and forget about Jack Higgins."

' "Perhaps I will," I said, and let him show me out.

'It had begun to rain and looked like it was set for the day. Nevertheless, I had resolved to find Jack and find him I would. Sherriff Wood was another long trudge across the moor but I did not let the rain deter me. I set off along Bridge Hill Road and then turned off onto the old sheep track that led up and over the hill and onto the moor.

'It was just as I was at my most exposed, picking my way through the gorse and bracken of the moor, that thunder clapped astonishingly loudly above my head and a bolt of lightning struck not fifty feet away to my right. My heart pounded and my skin was enlivened by the electricity in the air. I prayed then, prayed vigorously and passionately as my shoes filled with water and the continuous thunder shattered my nerves.

'I made the perimeter of Sherriff Wood a sodden mess, stripped of composure and longing for a bath and a warm fire. I knew roughly where the woodcutter's cabin was, close to Mary's Well and not much further, thank God. The shelter it could provide would be most welcome and so I forced myself on.

'The wood was dark and eerily still, despite the storm still raging above and beyond my sight. The birds had quietened their voices amid the tumult and every other living thing had apparently gone to ground. Only the shadows remained and fleeting glances of ghostly apparitions, as my mind played cruel games.

'Mercifully, I came upon the clearing quickly and the cabin that lay within it. I called out Jack's name but got no response. I called out again and again but to no avail and so decided to take shelter inside the cabin and wait out the storm. It was warm inside and dry.

'Though Jack was clearly not within, he or at least someone, had been present very recently. The stove had burning wood in its belly and there was unfinished bread and cheese on the table. I returned to the front door and looked outside but could see no trace of anyone and so decided to make myself at home and wait. I topped up the fuel in the stove, took off my sodden coat, hat, and shoes, and, though it felt a little inappropriate, ate some of the remaining bread and cheese. Feeling somewhat restored, I sat near the stove, pointing my cold feet towards the heat, and allowed my heavy eyelids to fall.

'Amongst my troubled dreams, a young girl of about

fifteen or sixteen appeared before me and spoke, her voice filled with menace.

'*You must sacrifice yourself,* she said, *for the good of us all.*

'Before I could respond, I was woken by the sound of the cabin door crashing open and there, framed in the doorway, stood Jack Higgins, axe in hand.

' "You shouldn't have come here," he spat. "You've brought it back!"

' "Jack, wait," I implored him. "I only wish to speak with you."

' "You brought it back!" he said again, as he advanced.

'My fear was now absolute. The man was clearly not to be reasoned with. His face was contorted with rage as he wielded his axe. He advanced towards me with hate-filled eyes, an animal-like growl exploding into a roar as he charged.

'I watched the axe sweep down, sharp blade brought unerringly towards my head. Falling backwards off my chair, I resigned myself to the inevitable. But it was only as my head hit the floor that I truly woke from my slumber to find myself alone, sweating and in a crumpled heap.

'In shock, I sprang to my feet, expecting an attack to come at any moment, but I was wrong. The cabin was cold and empty. The fire in the stove had long since died and there was no evidence of there ever having been food upon the table. I was still wearing the wet clothes I was sure I'd removed, and my head now throbbed in pain and utter confusion. It was time for me to leave. Never before had the idea of home felt so appealing. With great haste I left the cabin and re-entered Sherriff Wood in the direction I thought would lead me back towards the moor and Jessop's farm.

'I was running and scared when I burst into the small clearing that housed Mary's Well. It was there a new horror awaited me. For at the edge of the stone that encircled the lip of the well, lay Jack Higgins, bleeding into its gaping mouth. I knew Jack well enough to be quite certain it was indeed he who lay prostrate there, despite the fact his head was no longer present. The axe I'd witnessed in my dream lay at his side, stained with blood.

'I staggered in disbelief over to where he lay and prayed for his soul. As I did so, a voice I now recognised echoed from the well…

Sacrifice yourself, for the good of us all.

' "This is no sacrifice," I exclaimed into the trees, "this is murder!"

'I did not have the strength to move Jack's body but vowed to return with help. I set off once again for Jessop's farm, a ragged version of my former self.

'I stumbled across the heath, losing my shoes quickly to the eager peat bog made worse by the rain. But my discomfort was easily overshadowed by the desire to reach the safety of Jessop's farm and find some sanity there. I ran and fell onto hands and knees, picked myself up and ran again and yet I came no closer to my goal. I looked about me and the grey sky pressed down like a heavy weight upon my shoulders. A dense mist descended, robbing me of sight and reason.

Sacrifice yourself, for the good of us all, came the voice again, an echo from within the gloaming, and so I drove myself on, now almost blind and desperate. My strength had all but deserted me when I happened once more upon the sanctuary of the trees, but quickly realised there was no succour to be had there. For to my utter dismay, I could see that I had returned to Mary's Well. Jack's decapitated body was no longer present, nor was there any sign of it ever having been there. The axe was similarly gone, and no blood stained the earth or the well.

16

'I resolved to spend my remaining strength on disposing of the damned bottle down the well. Maybe it *was* cursed. I no longer cared. I removed it from my coat pocket and staggered over to the well with it clasped in my shaking hand. It was as I raised the thing above my head with no more thought than to cast it downward, that the apparition emerged from the mist. At first it *was* the mist, but as it flowed into the clearing, the shape formed into that of a young woman, dressed in peasant clothing. It was the girl from my dream.

' "Who are you?" I croaked. "And what do you want of me?"

' "When the plague came, they blamed it on me," she said.

' "Who did?"

' "The likes of you."

'I was confused enough already, but talk of the plague was nonsensical.

' "But that was three hundred years ago!"

' "Time has no meaning for me," she said. "I cannot rest. I must have revenge."

'I no longer believed my own senses, such was my confusion, but this apparition seemed real, or at least as real to me as Jack's body had been.

' "I can only surmise that I'm dreaming again, or lying on my bed delirious with fever," I said, "and so will consent to have this conversation with you before I wake and discover the truth. What makes you so sure that the blame was laid at *your* door?"

'The girl mocked me. "The truth? Ha! Well, they did burn me and place my remains in that bottle you hold so closely to your heart."

'I looked again at the bottle in disbelief, and renewed fear throbbed at my temples.

17

' "I see you're afraid," said the girl. *"They* were also afraid, afraid of the black death. It was I who suggested that all who suffered should sacrifice themselves, but only for the good of those that remained. It is true that I was considered a witch, but even my lore could not help those stricken with plague. Only fire can purge such a curse. But your Christian Church could see no further than Satan, and looked for his Mark upon me."

' "We are not all the same," I said.

' "No? Then how would you interpret the words of your God? *Thou shall not suffer a witch to live!"*

' "There are no true witches," I countered.

' "I have already told you that I am a witch. Do you doubt me?"

' "I do."

'The apparition drew closer, until I could see her eyes. They were as black as night. They looked into my soul and took hold of my will.

' "What do you want of me?" I begged.

' "Revenge!" she spat like a viper.

' "Take me then," I said, and the girl bared her teeth like an animal.

' "You will indeed be my instrument, Reverend Thomas Greenacre. Take up yonder axe!"

'I looked and there it was, once more by the well. I took it in my hands, no longer a man but as a vessel possessed… and from that moment, I remember no more…'

It is evident from this remark, that I have now completed my statement. The young constable lays down his notepad and pencil and looks aghast at his superior. His face is ashen. The inspector on the other hand stares at me with distaste. When he addresses me, I understand at once my fate.

'Though it is not for me to judge you, Reverend Greenacre, I believe you to be insane. Fortunately, you are lucid enough to be considered culpable for your foul actions

18

and will, if justice is properly served, pay the ultimate price. And may God have mercy on your soul.'

All I can do is nod my head in response. I no longer wish to live.

And now, as I write these final words, alone within my cold, damp cell, I have come to understand that in one respect at least, the inspector is quite correct. God alone will be my judge.

The rain beats down so hard and constant, the windscreen wipers of the Land Rover can no longer keep up. Jerry and Sarah have been on the road for hours and it's starting to get dark.

'We must be close now,' remarks a rather tired Jerry.

'I do hope so,' says Sarah, 'I'm starting to think this was a bad idea after all.'

They bounce up the track, thankful for the four-wheel drive. Finally, they pass a farm they recognise from a description in the book they are referring to. They turn uphill and spy their goal in the near distance.

'That has to be it,' says Sarah, pointing. Jerry smiles back at her.

The car slips and slides on the muddy surface of the track and Jerry engages a lower gear. The tyres bite and soon they emerge at the chapel gate and slide to a halt. Sarah is clearly excited. 'It's just as I thought it would be. Working in a museum has its advantages.'

Jerry turns off the engine. 'Tell me again what the book says.'

Sarah flicks through the pages and finds the place with the corner turned over. She begins to read the passage that has brought them here.

'The chapel, now derelict, has remained unused since the tragic events of 1876, when the Vicar, Reverend

Thomas Greenacre, violently murdered his parishioners during Sunday service, with an axe.'

'Good God,' says Jerry, 'that never ceases to amaze me. What on earth possessed the man?'

'A good question,' replies Sarah, 'and one I intend to use in my novel. Let's take a look around.'

They get out into the pouring rain and try the gate. It screeches open. They look at each other, grinning like school children, and hurry through. Skirting around the side of the chapel and into the small graveyard, they find a little shelter beneath an old oak tree. The area is unkempt, with nettles and briars everywhere and some of the gravestones have fallen. The chapel is clearly in a poor state, with many of the windows broken.

'Shouldn't you be taking some notes?' asks Jerry.

'Pictures will do,' replies Sarah, removing her phone from her jacket pocket.

'Perfect weather for a ghost story,' remarks Jerry, grinning.

Sarah ignores the comment, and wipes her rain-spattered glasses so she can see more clearly. 'I wonder if we can get inside.'

'Hang on,' replies Jerry. 'You didn't say anything about breaking and entering.'

'I don't think we'll need to do much breaking, do you?'

Sarah strides off towards a side door that looks the worse for wear. Jerry reluctantly follows. 'It won't take much, Jerry, go on.'

He instinctively looks around before giving the door a hefty kick. It yields easily. They hesitate for a moment or two before plucking up the courage to step across the threshold. The air inside is stale and a thick layer of dust covers every surface. There are birds in the rafters, or bats, they can't tell in the shadows.

'Jerry, this is where it happened. Right here!'

He nervously walks up the aisle to the dais at the front. A dusty bible is still spread open upon it. He blows off the dust and takes a look.

'Matthew, Chapter 2, the Slaughter of the Innocents,' he reads aloud.

'How very apt,' replies Sarah, taking more pictures.

Suddenly a dark shape flies down from the rafters and swoops towards Jerry's head.

'Shit!' he cries, waving his arms about.

The dark shape comes at him again and he sprawls forward, pushing the dais over with a loud thud, sending the bible skidding across the floor. Sarah comes running. 'Jerry! Are you OK?'

'Damn bird went for me,' he replies, wiping blood onto his fingers from his forehead.

'We must have frightened it,' says Sarah.

'Bloody frightened me,' he grumbles.

Jerry picks up the damaged dais and tries to put it back in place. As he does so, he notices a hole in the floor where it had been standing, obscuring its presence.

'Sarah, the dais was covering up a hole in the floor. Come and see.'

Sarah kneels down at the hole and uses the torch on her phone to inspect it. 'There's something in there,' she says, reaching in. She pulls out a velvet bag, tied closed with a woven cord. They look at each other with barely disguised excitement.

'Buried treasure now?' asks Jerry.

'Let's see,' says Sarah, as she undoes the cord. She puts her hand into the velvet bag and withdraws a silver bottle from within. They are speechless at their discovery. It is just as the book had described it. Finally, Jerry finds his voice. 'Could that really be…?'

21

Sarah replaces their find carefully back into the bag. 'We need to get this back to the museum. Time to go, Jerry.'

The rain is still falling in torrents as the Land Rover twists its way back down the hill. 'I can't believe it,' says Sarah.

'Put the radio on, Sarah, and find us some music,' replies Jerry. 'I need a distraction.'

Sarah turns on the radio but finds only static. 'It must be the weather,' she says, searching with the tuner.

The Land Rover skids, barely missing a tree. Jerry guns the accelerator and drives the car to safety. The weather seems to be getting even worse. 'That was a close one,' he gasps.

Then, out of the static noise a voice can almost be heard. Sarah tunes more finely and gradually it clarifies into the voice of a young girl. What she says strikes terror into their hearts as a lone figure emerges from the storm, on the road ahead, bloody axe in hand...

...*Sacrifice yourself for the good of us all, sacrifice yourself for the good of us all, sacrifice yourself for the good of us all*...

There is no one to hear them scream as their car spins off the road, tumbling away into the ravaged night.

The Story of Morgana Marestail

It was a time before the dawn of the second age of magic many centuries ago. The earthpower had slumbered for more than five hundred years. Those who struggled to keep the old religion alive passed on the knowledge of healing and herb lore from mother to daughter down the generations. One such daughter whose name was Morgana Fabbro lived in a small rural village, the identity of which has long since faded from memory. She was a girl of such great beauty that everyone who saw her marvelled and young men would travel from far and wide seeking her hand in marriage. But Morgana was betrothed already, to a handsome and good-hearted local boy whom she had grown up with and loved with all her heart.

Since being a little girl she had listened to her grandfather's stories of the great kings and queens of old and dreamed of a big impressive wedding with silk dresses, carriages, splendid food to eat and the best wine to drink. Unfortunately they were very poor. Her father was the local blacksmith, her mother the village healer and herbalist and the boy, Alfred, a farmer's son from the nearby hills.

She had spent many a happy day upon those hills, picking herbs and flowers and listening to the tuneful chatter of birds, but her mind always returned to her dream. It consumed her every thought, somehow diminishing the happiness that Alfred bestowed upon her with his love.

On her sixteenth birthday she finally decided, against her mother's wishes it must be said, to go and visit the local Lord who lived in a grand castle a few miles away and who owned all the land from the surrounding hills to the western sea. She intended to ask him if she could get married in his castle in return for the special knowledge of healing her mother had faithfully passed down to her.

When she arrived at the castle, she was dismayed to find that the Lord was in fact dying and would probably only last a few more days. However, when the Lord's son set his eyes upon Morgana, he fell immediately in love with her and asked her to marry him before even knowing why she was there. Morgana thanked the son for his kind offer but explained that she was betrothed already and had come seeking an exchange, her knowledge for the use of the castle in which to get married. She told him of her dream, her passion flushing her cheeks and misting her eyes in a way that made her appear even more beautiful. The son considered this for a moment and then quickly made up his mind to try and trick Morgana into marrying *him* instead.

'I will agree to your terms, Morgana, on two conditions,' he said.

'Anything!' replied Morgana eagerly.

'You must demonstrate your skills by healing my father,' the son continued, 'and, if you succeed, the castle, all its servants and fineries will be yours to use as you wish for one day. If you fail however, and my father dies, you will marry me instead and be my Lady. What say you?'

Morgana was terrified. Unlike his father, the Lord's son was well known to be a cruel and heartless man, feared by all whose paths crossed his. She also knew her skills were limited and there was a lot more yet to learn from her mother. She could tell from the hushed tones and sombre faces of those around her that the Lord was probably at death's door and may die before she could even begin to help. Yet the offer was too great to resist. The chance was there to fulfil her life's dreams and so, with trembling voice, she accepted the son's terms.

'I will need a day to collect healing herbs from the forest,' she said, 'and make the medicine your father needs.'

The Lord's son smiled, quietly satisfied with his own cunning. He felt sure his father would not even live that long and so, as soon as Morgana left, he began the preparations for his own wedding. He ordered the best wine be brought up from the cellars and set about instructing the kitchens to bake and roast food fit for a festival. Morgana returned home and told her mother what she had done. Her mother could see the fear in her daughter's eyes and felt sorrow at Morgana's plight.

'Tonight is a full moon my daughter,' she said. 'Go down to the pool at the centre of the wood and when the moonlight is reflected in it, pray to the Goddess for help. Here is what you must say:'

Diana, beautiful Diana!
Fair Goddess of the rainbow,
Of the stars and of the moon!
The queen most powerful
Of ancient lore made new!
I beg of thee Thy aid.
Show me how to conquer death,
Win back the Lord's last dying breath,
And marry then my life-long love,
And with Thy blessing from above,
The Witches' Gospel, I now pledge, to be ever true.

That night Morgana did as her mother had instructed. With her basket and knife for collecting herbs, she made her way to the pool at the centre of the wood and waited for the full moon to rise above the trees and cast its glowing face onto the surface of the still water. Morgana stood then at the edge of the pool and recited the words her mother had given her.

Just as she finished the prayer and opened her eyes she noticed something moving amongst the trees and then suddenly and very quietly, a beautiful, pure white horse emerged at the pool side to drink. However, before it could do so, the horse staggered and slumped down, snorting steam into the still night air.

Morgana could see now that the beautiful horse was injured. Red blood stained its moon-white mane and five deep crimson lines despoiled its noble neck... the marks of a hunter's claws. She raced around the pool to the horse's side filled with sadness and horror and at once forgot her own troubles and instead began to comfort the poor animal.

'Fear not, proud mare,' she said. 'I have knowledge of healing and will help you.'

At once she retrieved water for the horse to drink and then collected the herbs she knew would give the animal renewed strength. First Morgana made a poultice for the wounds and then she took a hair from the horse's own tail and, using the pin her father had made for her clothing, sewed up the poor creature's damaged neck. Soon after she was finished the horse rallied and stood up again shakily. It first nuzzled Morgana and then, with renewed vigour, whinnied into the ferns and trees of the wood as it slipped away and out of sight.

Morgana was alone again but just as she was gathering up her belongings, she heard a voice speaking to her. It tinkled musically like a stream and seemed to be coming from everywhere at once.

'*Morgana Fabbro, because you have forgotten your own troubles to help another creature in distress, you have shown yourself to be a true spirit, a child of the earth. I will therefore grant you the wish you so humbly prayed for. And from this day you will be known as Morgana Marestail.*'

'Thank you, thank you, thank you!' exclaimed Morgana. 'But pray tell me, what must I do to accomplish this task?'

'Take the herbs you gave to the wounded mare and mix with them the mushroom from beneath the oak tree. Add salt from the sea, ground chestnut, honey, verbena and water from this pool. Once the ailing Lord has drunk this brew, say again the words your mother gave you and he will rally. But be quick, he will soon be beyond your lore.'

Morgana did as the voice commanded and then ran all the way back home to collect from her mother's store what she could not obtain from the forest. With great haste Morgana then returned to the castle with her life-saving mix. The Lord's son was waiting for her as she entered the gates, breathless and flushed of face. He scoffed at her simple ingredients.

'Physicians from far and wide have administered to my father and yet he almost breathes his last. How then can this basket of weeds help him?'

'This is all I know,' replied Morgana shyly, 'so this I do.'

The son waved his hand dismissively. 'Make haste then,' he snapped, before seating himself at his father's desk.

Morgana sat down at the bedside of the Lord and deftly prepared her elixir as she had been instructed. The Lord's breathing was shallow and rattled in his chest. She carefully leaned over him and poured the liquid into his mouth, a few sips at a time. As she did so, she whispered the incantation into his ear noticing that his face was bright with moonlight from the window.

Then she waited, as did his son, servants and at least two physicians who stood scornfully looking on. They waited and they waited. As dawn began to break, the son's smile grew wider.

'It appears your magic has deserted you,' he said with some relish.

But just as he did so, the Lord's eyes opened for the first time in weeks.

'Water!' croaked the Lord. 'Water!' He coughed and spluttered.

Morgana beamed with a mixture of relief and gratitude but the son's face was like thunder. Not only did it appear that he had lost the woman he desired, he would not yet become Lord either.

'Get out!' he roared at the physicians and servants. 'Get out of my sight!'

Two days later the Lord, to the delight of his subjects, returned to something resembling health and Morgana, now called "Marestail", married her childhood sweetheart in the castle as she had always dreamed, with music, merriment and all the finery more befitting a princess than a blacksmith's daughter.

And so, with one act of faith and one act of kindness, earthpower was restored to the land and magic flourished once more amongst those who had stayed faithful to the old ways.

The Raven and the Witch-Pricker

(Based on the Newcastle Witch Trials of 1649)

In a pool of shadow I am, in raven form, waiting. The night is crisp with frost and our Earth Mother watches from her lofty throne, a limpid eye that illuminates the river like precious, shivering silk. I discern the forlorn cries of those condemned to die as they rise and fall on the chill breeze, and weep. My sisters? Perhaps, in one sense, and yet they are as innocent as I am not. They do not know the craft as I do, nor are they blessed with the *sight*. Or is it cursed? I can no longer tell the difference.

The Puritans have decided their fate by proxy, abdicating responsibility to a greedy Witch-Pricker whose pockets still jangle with the bones of those that did not bleed in Berwick. Twenty shillings per slim and fragile neck is a goodly return.

Souls for coals! Yes, at least here, where dusty stones as black as my borrowed wings matter more than pale flesh. Coal is a ruthless king that bows the backs of men and strikes the fear of God into the hearts of all dissenters. He will be worshipped with pick and shovel and human sacrifice.

I fly to the window now and peer with beady eye through iron bars into the gloomy, frigid cell. There they sit, old and young alike, cold, hungry, and consumed by a winnowing sorrow. I feel their thoughts as though they are my own, a swirling confusion of remembrance mainly. A few clutch at a fragile notion of past happiness, a lover's touch forever treasured, a child suckling at the breast, but most tremble in fear and hopelessness.

But hope is not extinguished all at once, like a snuffed candle. No, it first grows dim, as hunger bites and sickness walks like the Grim Reaper amongst those you care for. It fades a little more as cruelty and neglect take their savage toll and conflict rapes the future like a thief in the night. And here, amongst such women as these, the flame gutters and finally dies.

And the river flows on. Such a river as cares neither for milk nor honey, unless it can be traded. This is a man's river, the King's river, the old King, coal. There is prosperity to be had for those touched by that gritty finger of fate, whose fortunate births have placed them upon this earth as Lords, who raise their wealth from the ground and care not for those born to drag it out upon their backs.

Ah, the bitterness wells up in me as I watch these poor wretches wring their hands and sob, waiting for a morning that will herald little more than a final view of the Town Moor through the eye of a hangman's noose.

I squawk involuntarily and a girl looks up. She has the face of an older woman but is probably no more than twenty. Her eyes are ringed red and the moonlight pales her as though she were already a ghost. She stares at me blankly but I can sense her silent prayers. She asks for the wings of a raven to fly up and away into the night and then for forgiveness for such foolishness. She looks away, and the flame of hope winks out.

I cannot save you, my sisters, but I will take our revenge upon this, so called, Witch-Pricker. I swear to you by the Mother, he will not enjoy the fruits of his wicked calling. Though he may have pierced the flesh of many innocents already, I did not know of him in the Borderlands. Forgive me, my sisters, for if I had, I might have stopped him, smothered him in his sleep perhaps… but no, I could not have known. I must bide my time, but trust me sisters, it will be done.

I fly to the nearby tavern where I know he will be. The

windows glow amber from the fire crackling in the hearth as he sits alone, hunched over a flagon of ale, a less than pure Puritan. I study his face, as flickering shadows lick across his red-veined cheeks. His wits are dulled by the ale but I can still feel the lust, greed and self-satisfaction seeping from his sweating skin… the pride, the avarice. He is a foul man, a damaged man but crafty with it. He will not be easy to bring down. I must at least render him low; halt this rabid lust for pain and suffering, this hate of women. If I can shape it, I will bring him to the same end as his many victims, Mother willing.

I am silent and still, yet he has seen me or sensed me. He sneers in my direction, his wet, fleshy lips damp and slack, bloodshot eyes rheumy, crucifix falling about his chest, shimmering upon a stained tunic. It is a challenge… I hear it… feel it… and it is one that I accept…

The bird mocks me. It is no more than a smear upon the frosted glass and yet it mocks me. Evil always finds a way to rise again. It is no ordinary bird, no, but a foul spirit that chills me to the bone despite this fire. I can feel its knife-like talons upon my heart. A scream rises in my chest:
YOU HAVE NO POWER OVER ME!
And then it is gone. You have no power over me, I mumble, quietly reassured by the smooth warm cross between my fingers. More ale I think, much more…

I take to the sky again and soar ever higher. The town is laid out before me, the criss-crossing streets and alleyways obscured by a mix of smoke and shadow, where danger lurks like a golem raised from the mud. Ships, like monstrous ghosts, creak and groan against the jetties. But far above me, stars carpet the heavens like jewels. Yes, there is beauty in creation, all is not yet despoiled.

31

I see it now. I have waited and it has come again; the flame-red crescent over the eastern horizon, beyond the sea. The slumbering menace of a new day awakens and the fox once more leaves his lair in search of food. Soon the crowds will gather, soon the entertainment will begin.

I fly to the moor and alight upon the gallows. Only the hangman is present at this early hour. He flinches at the sight of me and throws a rock but I am too quick. I caw at him angrily and he backs away, the superstitious fool.

I cannot bear to stay, to witness this injustice. The creak of the rope, as it swings lazily on the breeze sickens me and I have seen it all before. The baying of the crowds, the abject fear of the women, the shuddering, twitching struggles of the dying, the cruel sights, the soul-shrivelling sounds and rank smells… they all disgust me. I have no need or desire to stay, but I will have my revenge…

I'm still drunk but must rouse myself. I know the smell of ale will be strong upon me but no matter. I do God's work and the Puritans can go to Hell with the witches as far as I care. I will see Satan's women hang and take my reward, and be damned those who claim them innocent. Most of them are better off dead anyway, filthy, vile creatures!

God speaks to me. In my troubled dreams I hear His voice calling me to this work, this righteous endeavour. No, my conscience is clear.

I will go now to greet the dawn and once this day is over I will move on to pastures new. I have chased the Devil from this dark and bitter town but to where? Not far I warrant. The raven will lead me there. Yes, I can taste it like a penny upon my tongue…

St Andrews churchyard is still and empty of life. I alight upon a gravestone close to the old stone wall where moss and lichen have long since taken hold. I will wait again as shadows stretch across the dewy grass, to mourn you, my sisters, as you return to our Mother and feed the earth with your innocent blood.

There will be no consecrated ground for you, no, nor stone or song to mark your passing. But I will know, and I will return, to the pit into which you are thrown as though diseased. I will remember you, my sisters, and pledge you this… to follow the Witch-Pricker to the ends of this world, and bring him to ruin!

I feel the shadow of the raven upon my neck, day after day, a brooding presence, forever at the edge of sight. My sleep is now troubled by a suffocating dread. How I crave to squeeze the life from this black tormentor with my own bare hands! I have taken to the roads and to the lesser paths of hills and valleys, and yet I cannot escape. My life is cursed; the Evil One has set his angel of death upon my heels. I live in constant fear, my bodkin concealed lest it reveal my calling. And yet I cannot bear to discard it, whilst hope remains.

And now, even the Church turns against me. Self-righteous fools who do not understand God's will, nor hear His voice as I do. They are men of power and influence and cannot be ignored. I sense their eagerness to destroy me, to cleanse their own guilt. It was they who sought my council, brought me into their midst to pronounce God's judgement. How they now shrink from all responsibility!

I have taken to the shadows, forced to skulk like a wild dog amongst the foetid underbelly of the streets. Only the raven sees me, only the raven caws with delight at my growing fear and calls down demonic prayers upon my head.

And now they come, the raven has brought the mob to end my pitiful life. Father, do not forsake your humble servant as he walks through the valley of the shadow of death…

I have whispered doubts into the minds of the high and mighty, my sisters, and set enlightened men upon this wretched creature that grovels before me, finally broken and bereft. He screams obscenities as he is dragged away by those who would see an end to him and his kind. I have haunted his every waking moment and cursed his sleep. And now, by his own kind he will be judged. On the morrow, those who once heralded his coming will drag him to the gallows, reviled and without dignity.

Revenge, though bitter-sweet, is mine, and yet it brings me little pleasure. I no longer have the heart for such dark matters. Though it remains my soul's desire to see an end to such mindless cruelty, I am weary of it all. Forgive me, as I now turn from this quest and set my troubled wings to loftier heights and my eyes to a new horizon. My heart longs to sup once more upon the beauty of this Earth. Farewell my sisters, my task for now is accomplished… farewell!

Blessed be.

The Clock Ticks

The clock ticks insistently as two men face each other across a chessboard. Being within an old library room, it stands comfortably amongst shelves of leather-bound books and Bentwood chairs. A small fire seethes in the grate.

A pale hand reaches forward and pinches the head of a knight, hesitating before sliding it into position. A younger man, contemplating the move, takes a sip of port. 'You're an old fool,' he says.

The air is dusty. Candles throw tendrils up walls. The young man presents a pawn to challenge the knight and lights a cigar. 'You don't mind do you?' He sees the older man lift one eyebrow and then take the pawn with his bishop. Casting his match into the fire, he surveys the board through a haze of fresh smoke. The older man appears implacable.

A young woman puts her head around the door. 'Are you coming to bed, darling?' she says.

'But I can't let him win,' replies the young man.

She looks troubled. 'You have to let him go darling; it's been almost a year now.' She gently closes the door.

The young man sighs. 'Good night father,' he says, knocking over his king.

The Calling

Part 1: The Crossing

From a land of mists she comes, morning dew clothing pale, translucent skin. Keen eyes flash like silver fish and chestnut hair falls about her face, reminiscent of autumn. Quietly she follows the satin ribbon of moonlight, through the ancient woods, and on towards the sea.

As a white hare she leaps forward, finding shelter behind a crag, whilst the lone wolf howls. Though her power flows from the earth, even she is wary of the underworld, for they will sense her, those dark and fathomless Watchers, ancient banes of tree and rock.

A ghostly light reflects from silver birch, illuminating the woodland and casting shadows that reach for her like talons. Wraith-like she flows between them, ever onward to the sea, and to that hidden tomb where the souls of her kin made their resting place. For this is the night of the Crossing, and she is called to set them free.

Part 2: The Watcher

Within the silent depths of this ancient wood, clothed in dewy moss and tangled roots, something stirs. As yet formless, dark and empty of soul and sight it waits.

Like smoke from dying embers it swirls and eddies amongst the knurled oaks, suddenly aware, sensing the distant souls of the lost and fallen. The appointed time has come and like a mute dog upon a leash it strains with silent screams, drinking the fear of countless dreams.

Cloaked in darkness, deeper than death, it slowly takes form, freezing the hearts of those who dare to bear witness within their troubled sleep; dripping dread like poison into their hearts.

And now, a storm gathers fury, electrifying the bruised sky and illuminating the Watcher, rising tree-like from the loam. The stench of decay hangs upon the energised air as this ancient curse gathers Earthpower from the slumbering soil. The taste of the witch is upon it, the one of whom the Fallen speak. It is the narrow Way she seeks, between the realms, and a Word of power to wake the dead. The scent of magic betrays her, and the Watcher follows the trace like a slavering dog.

Part 3: Silvanir, Guardian of the trees

In a time long before the age of man, when the Earthpower was yet a Word unspoken, the first trees stretched forth their limbs upon the land and breathed life into a fledgling world. And the Ancient of Days uttered the names of tree spirits and appointed them as Guardians of the forests, giving them authority over the new life that dwelled within.

But it is said that the Guardians are no more, their power diminished by saw, axe and fire, as the Earthpower stumbled with the coming of men. Yet now, as the trees scream and groan in protest at the rise of a Watcher, Silvanir, their last Guardian, hears those cries and opens his eyes once more.

He too senses the passing of the witch, flitting like moonlight amongst the saplings at the forest edge, and the stench of the Watcher as it bleeds life from all that it touches. He feels the approaching alignment that will open the Way and understands at once the great change that will claim them all.

Born of the first forest, his veins like the xylem and phloem of a rare flower, thriving beneath the dense, dark canopy, he hastens towards a final flourish. A fruitful life will be his gift to all the ancient brothers who once shared his calling, and to an age only the trees will remember. From a great oak he flows, as one made visible by his own choosing, and with his staff, goes forth to face the coming dread.

Part 4: The Healer

Though the earth tingles with life beneath the soles of her feet, she does not falter, for the Earth Mother has spoken and she must now obey. The path is clear, despite the storm that splits the sky from horizon to horizon. It is no ordinary fury unleashed upon the heavens, of that she is certain. There is old, dark magic at its heart.

She prays as she runs, and mingles her supplications with wild magic, so that she will not be hindered in her flight. The moon is no longer visible, nor the stars, but it does not matter. The heavenly bodies draw her forward like the rising sap flowing within roots, stems and branches.

She is the last of her kind, a Healer to this damaged land. Only she can summon the lore required to open the Way and direct the flow of Earthpower. It is a sacred calling, and one gladly accepted.

The appointed place is close now. She can taste salt within the rain that lashes at her face. The Way will open beneath the ancient Yew, where the Elders sleep, laid low by demon Hunters of old, in a time before the ice.

But there is also *wrongness* in the air, tainting the storm with blasphemy. She senses the pain of the trees as they weep in sorrow and knows it to be the foul work of a Watcher. She presses harder toward her goal, earth magic now turned ragged with exertion, and desolation close upon her heels.

Part 5: The forest trembles

Dark is the soul of a Watcher and darker still its intent. The forest trembles at its passing and withers at its touch. For it was made to punish the earth and infect the hearts of men with evil. Great power flows from another realm, driving the foul beast onward, endowing it with almost unlimited capability.

Yet into its path steps brave Silvanir, Guardian of the trees. He raises high his staff and calls upon the Earthpower, granted him by the Fathers of the Beginning. The air crackles as his staff burns with the runes of his lore. 'By the ancient wisdom of trees do I command thee,' he calls into the tortured sky, 'and by the healing gifts of nature do I forbid thee!'

The Watcher feels the earth magic diminish the dark flow that fuels its relentless progress. It gutters momentarily and is almost extinguished. Filled with hate and fury, the Watcher is forced to call upon its lord and master, and in so doing, feels the shame of weakness. 'My lord, do not forsake thy humble servant, for I am come to fulfil thy will within this land.'

With terrible ferocity the dark flow is restored and thrust upon Silvanir with unspeakable force. The Staff, hewn from the very tree of life, turns to ash in his hands and without it, his power is impotent. The Watcher reaches out a claw-like hand, plucking Silvanir's still beating heart from his chest, and taunts the stricken warrior. 'I now eat of your heart, but my master will feast upon your soul!'

Silvanir is cast aside like rotten wood, the last Guardian is fallen.

Part 6: The Temple of the Moon

Into the Temple of the Moon she hastens, as the Watcher approaches, now unhindered by the trees. Only the great

Waytree remains defiant, its portal poised and waiting for the coming of the One.

The altar is empty, but the memory of sacrifice lingers. For it is blood the gods demand, the precious elixir of life itself. And not just any blood will serve to quench their savage thirst, nor open the Way. Only the true magical bloodline will suffice. Only that which is of the Royal line, that rare and magical vintage will suffice. And so, as the heavens move once again into their favoured state, the Healer prepares to become the Lamb.

The fury of the storm is now spent and the moon is full and bright as she slips the obsidian blade from her belt. It is an artefact of great and noble heritage, imbued with the subtle lore of her forefathers. Hesitating, she tests the edge of the blade against her pale flesh and feels it yield to the lightest of touches. It will be an easy and pure act of love, though fear is ever present.

But even now, as the moment draws close and slumbering ghosts moan upon the breeze that flirts with stone and sea, the Watcher casts a deep shadow across the moonlit scene. With Words of power it stays the Healers hand, as the heavens combine to finally make possible the narrow Way. The time will soon pass, the moment forever lost.

Yet she has also been granted a Word, a treasured gift that only now takes on true significance. She utters the Word as though she were a songbird caught up in the thrill of a summer's morning, and with that sweet chime, the Watcher's hold is broken.

The obsidian blade whispers death upon her veins, and from the ancient temple grounds a great beam of frosted light rises triumphantly into the night sky. Heaven and Earth are conjoined once more as mother and child, blessed and favoured.

As she becomes ever paler and autumn turns to winter upon her fragile form, the Healer witnesses the first of her kin step out from the standing stones of the Temple and is filled with overwhelming joy. For on this night of Crossing, she alone was called to set them free.

Epilogue

Think not of sacrifice, nor of loss, for the Earth is filled with the light of magic and darkness has not overcome it. Though the forest may tremble, its spirit remains strong, emboldened by the wisdom of the few, born to preserve the breath of life, the new Guardians of Earthpower.

Do not fear the Watchers but be ever vigilant and prepare your Words of power, for the day may come when this fragile world whispers *your* name upon the breeze and your roots will be tested against the rising storm.

Until then, tread lightly upon the forest glade and mindfully amongst your fellows, for there is beauty to be had there, and freedom to be shared. Do not be troubled or overshadowed by fear, for the Earthpower yet lives and is freely given.

Love much and judge not, for with love the Earthpower is sustained and with judgement comes only bitterness and resentment. May your roots be firm and deep and your limbs ever reaching for the sky.

The Bogeyman

Prologue

It is Halloween, and within the silent depths of an ancient wood, clothed in dewy moss and tangled roots, something stirs. As yet formless, dark and empty of soul and sight it waits.

Like smoke from dying embers it swirls and eddies amongst the knurled oaks, suddenly aware, sensing the distant souls of the lost and fallen. The appointed time has come at last and like a mute dog upon a leash it strains with silent screams, drinking the fear of countless dreams.

Cloaked in darkness deeper than death, it slowly takes form, freezing the hearts of those who dare to bear witness within their troubled sleep; dripping dread like poison into their blood.

And now, a storm gathers fury, electrifying the bruised sky and illuminating the golem, rising tree-like from the loam. The stench of decay hangs upon the energised air as this ancient bane takes a first lumbering step and then another, eager for the destruction it has been created to unleash. It is the children of this world the creature has been called to punish, for the sins of the fathers who turned their faces from the light.

A deep and ominous rumble claims the night, groaning and straining until finally it fractures into a thunderclap, waking a thousand restless souls in unison, gasping from their tormented dreams. All have heard the same three dread words, echoing from a dark dimension…

I… am… come.

Victor had been told many times by his mother that the bogeyman was an invention and didn't really exist, and yet he just couldn't bring himself to believe her. This was very confusing to Victor. In all other things he trusted his mother implicitly and without question, as is common with an only son, but in this matter he was conflicted.

You see, last year, last Halloween actually, Victor had been out in the neighbourhood trick or treating, dressed as a rather splendid vampire, and had found himself temporarily separated from his friends. He'd been lagging behind, checking his treats, and absentmindedly crossed the quiet street which backed onto Birling Wood. He didn't notice the others getting invited into The Vicarage for apples and sweets, so when he looked up all he could see were the scary shapes of ink-black trees and the shadows cast by the nearby orange streetlight.

During the day, the woods were great fun. There were trees to climb, bird nests to filch and plenty of ugly insects to catch and put in jars. But at night, especially a moonless one such as this, the woods became a place of ghostly visions.

Victor turned full circle looking for his friends, but discovered he was alone on a street of large Victorian houses with long. dark drives and tall hedges.

He was about to head off towards one of them, when he first heard it. It was like a hoarse whisper, swirling past his ears... *Victor... I see you Victoooorrrrr.*

'Who's there?' he snapped. 'If that's you. Smithy. I'll give you such a smack.'

Come to me Victor, for I am yet weak and cannot come to you.

The whispering voice circled around Victor as though carried on a breeze, and yet the night was still. It seemed to draw him on, into the woods and he had to fight to resist it.

'No I will not!' he cried. 'I'm going home!'

Come to me, Victor, I have something of great value to give you... come.

Victor staggered, took a single step into the woods, and noticed a deeper darkness engulf the trees and shrubs ahead of him. He took another step and then another, as fear knotted and churned his stomach.

It was just as he began to fade away into those curiously hypnotic depths that a car pulled up on the road behind him. At the edge of his senses, he heard the clunk of a door and then a familiar voice. It was his mother.

'Victor! Is that you? What on earth are you doing? Come here at once!'

His dream-like trance broken, Victor turned and ran to his mother, grasping her around the waist in relief. Once back in the safety of his home, he'd tried to explain the strange occurrence but his mother hadn't believed him, though he pleaded the truth of it.

And now, here he lay, a whole year later, in the semi-darkness of his room, remembering. On an impulse, he got up and went to the window. He could just about see Birling Woods from here, across the common and over the rooftops. His heart skipped a beat as a crow flew past the window like a missile, making him jump.

The wind was getting up and grey clouds scudded across the dark blue backdrop of the sky, illuminated by an impressive full moon. It seemed to stare down at Victor like an all-seeing eye, turning the grass of the common into a white satin sheet.

It was then Victor noticed the lone figure standing in the field, watching him. He gasped and stepped back in fear. *It couldn't be a person*, he thought, *much too big to be a man.* The figure seemed almost tree-like, rooted, watching. And then the familiar whisper emerged once again, as though from the air of his room, and a fresh horror gripped him like a taloned hand.

Tonight, Victor… tonight I bring you my gift.

He pulled the curtains together and peeped through the crack, his short rapid breathing rattling in his chest. The figure was gone. His eyes went wide as he scanned the common for any sign of it, but there was none.

'Mum,' he called out weakly. 'Mum!' he shouted, finding his voice.

Victor's mother opened the lounge door with an audible sigh, ghostly blue light from the TV escaping into the hallway. 'Go to sleep, Victor!' she scolded.

'I can't,' he replied. 'I keep hearing voices and there's something creepy outside.'

'Don't be ridiculous, Victor, it's just the TV you can hear, and it's Halloween for goodness' sake. There will be plenty of folk dressed up tonight... now, go, to, sleep!'

Victor swallowed hard and climbed back into bed, pulling the covers up over his head. He felt hot and sweaty and a million miles away from sleep.

Oh, I can see you, Victor, came the creepy voice once again. *You cannot hide from me, boy.*

Victor shot out of bed and ran to the bedroom door, intending to run downstairs. Facing his mother's anger seemed an acceptable price to pay for her protection from whatever it was trying to play tricks on him. He would pretend to be sick. After all, the sweat was now pouring down his back.

Victor grasped the door handle and pulled, but to his horror it wouldn't budge. The door was jammed shut and try as he might he just couldn't open it.

'Mum!' he shouted again. 'Mum, I'm not feeling well.'

This time Victor's mother didn't answer.

'Mum! Mum!'

No reply.

It was then he heard it... the *ticky–tap–tap* on his window. The *scrapey, scratchy, ticky–tap–tap.*

Victor froze. He stared at the curtains and held his breath.

Ticky-tap-tap... ticky-tap-tap.

Slowly Victor persuaded his feet to move. Trembling like an autumn leaf, he shuffled back towards the window.

Ticky–tap–tap... ticky–tap–tap.

'Who's there?' he croaked.

Ticky–tap–tap... ticky–tap–tap was the only response.

Victor reached out a shaking hand to the curtains and, with a sudden surge of bravery, swept them open, only to reveal a sight that caused him to gasp and take a step back.

Bizarrely, a new tree stood in the garden, looming large and imposing in the flickering moonlight. It was now raining and a strong breeze buffeted the finer branches of this new, and yet ancient-looking oak, against his window.

Ticky–tap–tap... ticky–tap–tap.

'But that's impossible,' he said, out loud.

Open wide your window, Victor, came the voice again, *for I have something to give you.*

'I will not!'

Do not be frightened, Victor, come, open your window.

'No!'

Then I must come to you in anger!

The breeze grew stronger and became a wind, and then a storm. Rain lashed upon the windowpane like ball bearings and branches whipped the glass like the cat-o-nine-tails he'd seen on a pirate film during the summer holidays.

Victor screamed and fell to his knees. He thought for sure the noise would at last bring his mother, but still she didn't come.

All at once the window shattered spraying shards of

glass everywhere. The curtains billowed inwards with the fury of the storm and with a sound like wood yielding to the axe, the branches of the tree entered his room as the arms of a hideous monster.

The next morning Victor's mother called him down to breakfast in the usual way. When he didn't respond she stomped upstairs to scold him, only to find his empty bed neatly made and his school uniform placed carefully on his chair as always. She wasn't at all sure whether to be concerned or irritated.

'Victor? Victor where are you? We don't have time for this, my boy. You will be late for school.'

When there was still no reply, she went back downstairs to look for him. It was certainly out of character for Victor to play silly games like this.

'Victor... Victor!'

Victor's mother looked everywhere, but to no avail. Finally, she went out into the garden, thinking he may have gone to the shed where he kept his bike.

She noticed it as soon as she opened the door, right in the centre of the lawn as though it had always been there... a healthy, strong, young oak tree, stretching out its branches. It was more than a sapling, yet not quite a tree. She walked around it, puzzled by its presence and it seemed to shiver and rattle its leaves as she did so.

'Well I never,' she remarked out loud. 'Where on earth did that come from?'

The Afterlife of Jacob Hardy

It was the last thing Jacob Hardy expected of the afterlife. He'd thought about heaven and hell of course. Doesn't every dying person? Even a non-believer must wonder, as they slip away, where they might be heading next, if indeed their life's assertions proved to be incorrect.

Jacob had been brought up by his strict, Presbyterian mother, as a Christian, with strong ideas about immortality. But as with many religious people, nagging doubts were never far away from the surface. However, for Jacob, the notion of an afterlife was ingrained into his psyche, immovable. The doubts he experienced were seldom about that immutable fact, but rather about the true nature of God.

He'd always thought it most unlikely that God would turn out to have much resemblance to the one worshipped so earnestly by his mother, but as to a reliable alternative, he had little to offer. And so, as his mortal eyes closed for what he believed to be the final time, he was genuinely surprised to open them again sat in a wingback chair, next to a wooden cot in which lay a sleeping baby.

'Well I never,' he exclaimed. 'What on earth am I doing here?'

'A very good question, Jacob Hardy,' came the unexpected reply, from somewhere behind his right shoulder.

Jacob turned his head to see, standing over him, a thin, pale and very naked man. He was hairless and gaunt yet strangely handsome.

'Who are you?' Jacob asked.

'Another reasonable question, but who or what I am is not important right now. The important questions are surely where and why?'

'Very well,' replied Jacob, 'where am I and why am I here?'

'That's more like it. You, my late friend, are in a small rural village in the Highlands of Scotland and the baby before you will be named Ruth. You, to put it quite simply, have been assigned as her guardian angel.'

Jacob was astonished. 'But, but, I'm not worthy of such a thing. I've had doubts; I've been... less than perfect.'

'You don't need to tell me,' said the pale man, 'I was there, every step of the way. I saw what you did on your eighteenth birthday.'

Jacob visibly shrank in his chair.

'Don't worry, I did a lot worse,' chuckled the man. 'This is your chance to prove yourself worthy, make that difference in the world you've always craved.'

Just then, the bedroom door opened and a young woman came in. Jacob gasped, certain that he was about to be discovered and subsequently become the subject of much consternation, but it quickly became apparent that he was invisible. The woman simply smiled down at the baby and tucked in her blanket, without so much as a glance in Jacob's direction.

'All good, David,' she called out in hushed tones, 'she's fast asleep.'

The young woman then kissed her hand and pressed it to the baby's cheek before leaving.

'But I don't know how to be a guardian angel,' pleaded Jacob, quailing at the responsibility.

He'd never been good at taking charge, more of a follower than a leader. Fiskale & Findlay Accountancy firm had been his lot in life, man and boy. It is certainly correct that he'd desired to make a difference in the world, but then again, he'd never had the courage. It was simply the dream he occasionally allowed himself, over coffee and biscuits at his desk, with the cherry blossom tree in full bloom drawing his gaze through the office window. He'd not been a father either. A few nephews and nieces were the closest he'd been to children. The thought of taking responsibility for the welfare of such a creature appalled him.

'Then you had better learn fast,' replied the man. 'Once the girl has been baptised, it's over to you.'

'And when is that?' asked Jacob, staring in wonder at his new charge.

'Next Sunday morning,' came the reply, and the pale man promptly disappeared.

'Hang on a minute!' spluttered Jacob, as the baby stirred.

Jacob looked on as the baby's restlessness gravitated into squirming and remembered something from his distant childhood.

'Rock-a-bye baby,' he sang, rather awkwardly, 'on a t-tree t-top.' But to no avail. The baby grumbled noisily, kicking off her blanket. Jacob tried another song, in a tremulous voice…

'Bye, b-baby bunting, daddy's g-gone a hunting…'

The grumbling escalated to a snotty cry that grew louder and louder by the second as Jacob danced from one foot to the other, wondering what to do. Mercifully, the young woman reappeared and swept the baby up into her arms.

'What's wrong, my darling? Are you hungry?'

The baby, now in full cry, howled and squirmed as Jacob looked on, utterly bemused. 'Oh dear,' he groaned, 'oh dear, oh dear.'

The baptism was a small, family affair, held in the local kirk, which was located on a hill at the edge of the village. Jacob watched in bewilderment as the vicar conducted the service with practiced ease. He'd never felt more awkward whilst attending church. The reasons for this were many, but foremost in his mind was the fact he was now completely naked, as the pale man had been. He realised, of course, that he couldn't actually be seen, but still felt compelled to cover his nether regions with his hands. He'd tried to pick up a bible to act as cover but his hand went straight through it. Anyway, placing a bible on your private parts didn't seem altogether appropriate to Jacob either. His mother would be appalled.

Baby Ruth, for her part, seemed to stare straight at him, with a look, that to Jacob, resembled disdain or at best morbid curiosity. Her eyes seemed to follow him wherever he stood and so he hid, behind the rather prim looking organist, finding it remarkably amusing to sit upon the keys she was playing.

As the service drew to a close, the pale man suddenly reappeared, at his side.

'All yours now, Jacob,' he said.

'But I don't know anything about children,' begged Jacob.

The pale man sighed. 'You don't need to. Just be there when she needs you most. A nudge here and a nudge there will do, nothing too radical.'

Jacob was confused and frustrated by his new circumstances, and now this pale chap's attitude rankled too. Uncharacteristic sarcasm bubbled to the surface.

'What should I do when everything is going along nicely then? Just hang around with no pants on?'

The pale man replied as though speaking to a child. 'That's not how it works, Jacob. There's a fair bit of singing involved.'

'Singing?'

'Yes, singing, with the heavenly host. Unless you can

play the harp of course. There's always a special place for harp players.'

'Harp was never my first instrument,' said Jacob, now wielding sarcasm like a weapon. 'And I'm not exactly the great Caruso in the singing department either.'

'I see,' replied the pale man, sounding disappointed. 'How about praise?

Jacob thought about this for a moment. 'Well, I've never been the overly critical type,' he replied.

'Not that kind of praise,' said the pale man, with just a hint of exasperation. 'God doesn't need anyone to simply tell him what a fine job he's doing. I mean worship, adoration. Think you can manage that?'

'Well, yes, of course,' replied Jacob, feeling a little abashed. *Mother would not have appreciated me doing anything other, of course I can bloody worship,* he thought and wished he had the courage to say.

'Good. We'll let you know when Ruth needs you. Until then, let me introduce you to the worship and adoration group.'

And with that, both men disappeared.

Jacob hadn't spent much time with Ruth until she was five years old and on a shopping trip with her mother in Inverness. They were heading for Eastgate Shopping Centre, hand in hand. He'd been practicing his glorifying when a tingle went up and down where his spine used to be, alerting him to some forthcoming need of his presence.

He emerged on the corner of Church Street and watched them approaching. Ruth was clutching a doll in one hand and her mother in the other. Jacob thought she looked very sweet indeed as she skipped along in black, patent leather shoes.

Remarkably, Ruth seemed to look straight at him as they passed.

'Mummy,' he heard her say.

'Yes darling?'

'Why was that man not wearing any clothes?'

Ruth's mother stopped and looked back.

'What man darling?'

'He was over there by the clothes shop,' replied Ruth, pointing.

'Oh, that would just be a mannequin waiting to be dressed, not a real man,' said her mother.

'What's a manikin?'

'A dummy, the sort they put clothes on to show how they look. Like a big doll.'

'Was not,' said Ruth, sulkily. She tried to pull her mother back towards Jacob.

Jacob could see Ruth's mum was looking hassled and in no mood to humour her daughter any further.

'Come on, my darling, let's just get to the shops and find somewhere to buy a drink. Then we can find Daddy a birthday present.'

'Can I have Coke?' asked Ruth.

'Maybe lemonade,' replied her mother.

Ruth reluctantly agreed and on they continued.

It was then Jacob noticed another naked man at the bus stop, staring at Ruth in a most peculiar way. Nobody noticed *him* either. This was most confusing to Jacob. Surely the girl would only be assigned one guardian angel? He approached the man from behind and tapped him on the shoulder. The man looked around at Jacob and sneered.

'Oh, it's you,' he said.

Jacob was taken aback by the curtness of this stranger.

'And who might you be?' he asked.

'They didn't tell you?'

'Indeed they did not.'

The man tutted. 'Simon's the name and making mischief is my game.'

'Mischief?'

'Yes and a bit of mayhem if I can get away with it.' The man looked quite pleased with himself.

Realisation began to dawn on Jacob. 'Wait a minute,' he said, 'are you telling me you're a... a demon?'

'A bit slow aren't you?' drawled the man. 'Trainee demon actually, but don't think you're going to get all your own way with young Ruth there, angel face.'

'You stay away from her... or else!' snapped Jacob, suddenly becoming extremely cross.

'Or else what?' replied the sneering Simon.

'Just, just you wait and see what,' replied Jacob, as the trainee demon disappeared with an audible pop.

For Jacob, this changed everything. He was going to have to pay a lot more attention from now on. Ruth and her mother were now out of sight, and so was Simon. Anxiety churned his phantom stomach as he rushed to find them.

Ruth and her mother were sitting in a café when Jacob reappeared. Ruth was drinking lemonade through a straw and looking rather sulky.

'But why couldn't I have cola, Mummy,' she whined.

'You know why,' replied her mother, 'it makes you naughty,'

'Does not!' grumbled Ruth.

Just then, Simon appeared at Ruth's shoulder and whispered something into her ear. Jacob watched in horror as Ruth filled her straw with lemonade and squirted it on her mother's mobile phone which sat on the table in front of them.

Ruth's mother slapped her handbag down onto the table and angrily mopped up the mess with a tissue. 'You naughty girl! That's the last time you get *any* sort of sugary drinks from me. Just wait until I tell your father.'

Ruth stared in disbelief at what she had done. Her father would be so disappointed in her and that was the worst thing ever. She had absolutely no idea why such things kept happening. After the cola incident with the goldfish she'd promised to be good and really meant it, but that was only last week and already the promise was broken. She sighed and puffed out her cheeks as her mother tried to clean up the sticky mess.

Simon on the other hand was giggling, looking extremely satisfied and it was clear to Jacob just what was going on.

'You rotter,' he said to Simon.

'Thank you,' he replied.

Jacob tried to look intimidating but couldn't quite manage it.

'I'm going to have to keep my eye on you,' he said, pointing.

'If I had any boots I'd be quaking in them,' replied Simon, and then promptly disappeared again.

Jacob was to have many battles with Simon over the coming months and years, usually revolving around those choices that every person makes as they grow up, such as whether to tell the truth when a lie is so much easier. Whether to say that thing you know will hurt or stay silent, whether to believe in yourself or choose to despise your own failings. Such matters troubled Ruth greatly as Jacob and Simon struggled constantly for supremacy.

Occasionally, Ruth would stare in their direction, squinting as though she could almost, but not quite see them. 'It's all *your* fault!' she would complain when something else went wrong. Jacob instinctively knew that she at least *felt* their presence, although they became more and more indistinct as Ruth grew older. Once, Jacob overheard Ruth tell her best friend that she had a guardian angel.

'But he's useless,' she continued, and Jacob agreed.

However, the biggest and most important battle came when Ruth was about to turn sixteen. Things had been going quite well in the main. School was fine, as were relationships with friends, but unfortunately Ruth and her mother had not been getting on well at all. The latest argument had occurred over plans for a birthday party. Ruth wanted to go out to town with her friends and stop over at someone's house. Whereas her mother was anxious about that and insisted on a family do with just a few friends involved. Neither could see the other's point of view and as usual, this resulted in shouting and the slamming of doors.

To Jacob's disgust, Simon had taken advantage of this and contrived that she should meet an older boy from a neighbouring town, who owned a car and had a job at the local fisheries. They had secretly been seeing each other for weeks, driving around with the boy's older friends in noisy gangs.

Ruth's mother eventually found out and, being very wary of a boy who was well known to have a rather chequered past, banned her daughter from seeing him anymore. Despite Jacob's best efforts, Ruth and the boy had now decided to run away together. He was a charismatic and very persuasive boy, the sort that every young girl dreamed of and every parent feared.

Jacob stood by sadly as Ruth stuffed items of clothing into a holdall.

'Oh dear,' he said. 'Oh dear, oh dear, oh dear.'

'Admitting defeat, angel face?'

Simon had reappeared at Jacob's side and was looking smug.

'I've warned you before about calling me that,' said Jacob, through gritted teeth.

'Ah, if only she'd gone for that nice boy from church group eh, angel face?'

'At least Robert is the same age and from a nice family!' retorted Jacob in frustration.

'Exactly,' replied Simon, 'boring.'

Jacob ignored the jibe and whispered second thoughts into Ruth's ear. She paused and sat down heavily on her bed. Angus was handsome and very grown up, a bit scary, yes, but in a good way. But her dad would be so disappointed and that made her very sad indeed.

'Oh no you don't,' said Simon, stepping into the breach. 'Your mother makes your life hell,' he whispered at Ruth, and the spell slipped into her mind like poison.

Ruth began packing again, angrily stuffing the bag to bursting.

Jacob looked around for inspiration and spotted the stack of books teetering on the edge of a shelf. He caused them to fall loudly, knocking over a few other things as they fell.

'What's going on up there?' shouted Ruth's Mother.

'Nothing!' she replied.

'Well keep the noise down or it will be lights out, do you hear me?'

'Yeeees!'

Ruth then noticed one of the books that had fallen to the floor. It was the one she'd received for good attendance at Sunday school years ago, *Shadow the Sheepdog* by Enid Blyton. It made her think of Robert. He was a pain in the neck, following her around all the time like a puppy. But no matter how horrible she was to him, he always came back for more.

'You crafty bugger,' said Simon.

Jacob smiled, quietly pleased with himself. It might have worked too, if Simon hadn't anticipated the move and encouraged Angus to come early. The sound of small stones hitting her bedroom window heralded his arrival. She rushed to the window and opened it.

'Quiet you idiot,' she called out, grinning from ear to ear.

Angus smiled up at her winningly and suddenly there seemed to be no going back. Ruth threw down her bag and held up her hand, indicating she'd be five minutes. *Now for the note.*

She held pen over paper with trembling hands.

'You'll break their hearts,' whispered Jacob, and her eyes brimmed with tears.

'A desperate move,' said Simon, but Jacob *was* desperate. He quickly whispered again.

'Angus doesn't love you, but your parents do, even your mother.'

'Your mother hates you,' whispered Simon. 'Remember how she humiliated you in front of your friends… forced you to take off that skirt you loved? Refused to let you go to that festival?'

I've decided to leave home, she wrote, *I will be OK so don't worry. Please don't try to find me. I will write soon. Ruth.*

She placed the note on her pillow and crept down stairs. Her parents were watching TV in the front room. The flickering light was hypnotic. They seemed so detached from her at that moment.

'How could you hurt them like this? You are their only child,' whispered Jacob, frantically.

Ruth was paralysed by indecision. Her heart thumped erratically as she stood transfixed by her whirling thoughts.

'It's now or never, you know that,' whispered Simon.

'You need more time to think things through,' whispered Jacob.

'A man like that won't hang around,' whispered Simon.

'He will if he really loves you,' whispered Jacob.

'Why take the chance?' whispered Simon.

'Don't break your dad's heart,' whispered Jacob.

And that was the whisper that worked. Just as the angel's breath washed over her, Ruth's dad laughed at something on the TV. Jacob hoped it would remind her of all the times they'd laughed together and make her realise that she simply couldn't go through with it. He was right. She turned then and went back upstairs, crumpled the note and threw it in the wastebasket.

The sound of another stone hitting the window reminded her of Angus. She went to the window and looked down at him standing there in the half-light. He looked irritated.

'What's keeping you?' he rasped.

'I'm sorry Angus, I just can't. Let's talk about it tomorrow.'

'For goodness sake, Ruth, haven't we discussed it enough already!'

Ruth could see how angry he was. There was no talking to him when he got like this. She closed the window and sighed, watching him stomp away along the gravel path. When she turned, her father was stood in the doorway.

'Oh, hi Dad.'

'You OK, Pumpkin?'

'Yes, why?'

'No reason. Just thought I heard a noise outside.'

Ruth looked at her feet and said nothing, tears now flowing freely down her cheeks. Secretly, her dad was aware of her inner turmoil.

'Come here, Pumpkin,' he said, with open arms. And she did.

'I suppose you think you've won,' moaned Simon.
Jacob was doing a little dance of joy that infuriated the demon. Simon quickly disappeared again with his customary pop, to be replaced by the pale man.
'You did well,' he said to Jacob.
'Thank you,' he replied, 'I did, didn't I?'
The pale man smiled. 'I've been instructed to tell you something quite splendid.'
'And what might that be?'
'You've earned your wings.'
As the pale man said this, angel wings began to sprout from Jacob's back. Within moments he could spread them out majestically, or retract them at will. He glowed with pride.
'Well, I never,' he said, astonished.

Styx

I am alone. I have brought myself here, amongst heather and hill, where solitude is a natural state. The mist has rolled in from the sea, obscuring everything. The birds are silent, and my breathing rasps loudly in my ears. I step out and walk down the familiar track to the loch, my clothes damp. Little prisms of water cling to my beard like the spiders webs that glisten in the bushes lining my path. It feels like I'm breathing water and old fears resurface.

I count my steps. By three hundred I've reached the fallen tree and pause, listening. A woodpigeon snaps noisily through the upper branches of the canopy I know is there, but which remains opaque to my sight. If anything, the mist thickens, finding the interstices of my woollen sweater as though it were moss.

Five hundred and sixty steps and the track divides. I turn right and feel the familiar pull on my legs that reminds me I'm heading down towards the shore. My feet slip a little on the now slick, compacted soil and I become more cautious, occasionally turning sideward to get a better grip with my boots.

I can hear the water now, lapping languidly over the pebbled edges of the tiny bay that is my goal. It is close, and as the mist swirls, it momentarily thins, revealing the small boat tilted against a tangle of bushes and alder saplings. It is where I left it long months before, as I'd hoped it would be, though God knows how.

You are with me, passive, an observer, no more than that. Invisible to sight, and yet not to smell. The piney, loamy scent of the woods is reminder enough, but beyond that, invading my senses as I yield to the memory, is the perfume impregnated into my skin, my sodden clothes, the glorious essence of… you. A tiny particle of joy enters my nose and lingers, lasting long after your features have blurred in my mind's eye. It is that mote of ghost-like fantasy that deposits me here, obscured by mist as though in a dream.

I'm shaking, unsure whether it's the chill air or the anticipation that claims me as I crunch and squelch onto the shore. Within moments my hand finds the smooth, painted surface of the boat, which gives slightly under my weight. 'I'm here,' I say out loud and my voice is that of a stranger.

I trace the shape of the boat and find the prow where I know it is secured and free it once more. Climbing in, I find the oars submerged in ankle-deep water and use one to force the boat back and out of the shallows. And now, I drift silently as though upon a millpond, reflecting.

I decide to secure the oars and strike out. I pull with all my strength, pull and pull until my arms ache and the oars slash raggedly at the oily, almost turgid surface of the loch. I pull and pull until my lungs burn and shoulders scream and still I pull. I call out, 'Where are you?' And the sound collapses upon me, compressed. The anger, the self-pity is thrown back into my face. I close my eyes and the world turns red and featureless.

Inertia drives the boat on but I am no longer able to row. It slows and will soon stop. It has no life of its own, only that which I give it and I have no more to give. My hand trails in the water and I welcome the touch as though it were that of an old friend. I look for you in the mist, as the wan light illuminates the shivering air, but you do not come. I close my eyes once more and you appear as a flickering image, as though in an old time movie. You're smiling, you were always smiling. Even during those crushing days when I'd lost you before you were truly gone.

'If you will not come to me then I will come to you,' I whisper, and like a wraith, I slip into the water. My heart pounds as I dive deeper and deeper into the shadows from which I know I will not return. This alien world, in which I now trespass, fills my mind with waves of fear that flow in elegant tides behind my eyes. And then, a new thought strikes me, and I wish with all my heart I could open my mouth and laugh out loud. For as the moment draws nearer and the darkness becomes like a gloved hand upon my face, I realise with such certainty, with such overwhelming conviction, that I have never felt more alive.

Song of the Rolling Sea

The girl stood amongst coarse dune grass, her gaze set to the horizon. *The light is different here*, she thought, focussing on a small sailing boat close to Coquet Island, about a mile offshore. *The sky is different too.*

Back in her hometown, the sky had often seemed as filthy as the street, a constant reminder of her childhood in the city. But here, surrounded by hills and sea, heaven smiled down, filling her vision with feathery clouds that fanned out like giant seagull wings.

They brought her here, to this other world, at the start of summer. The new people seemed nice. It was an inadequate word, but it summed things up in her head. Like most foster parents they were full of smiles and unnecessary accommodations, but meant well and pretended not to notice her quiet, introspective moods.

She hadn't even heard of Alnmouth before she'd arrived on the train from London, but as they'd pulled into the station on that sunny day in May, the view of the village with its twinkling water and colourful houses had quickly captured her imagination. It felt like a fairy tale waiting to be written. Even Jo, the stern-faced care manager, seemed impressed as they gazed out from grime-streaked train windows across the estuary, where small boats bobbed and gulls soared in noisy gangs.

'Just look at that,' she'd remarked, and felt another pang of anticipation rise in her chest.

And now here she stood, in late summer, attuned to this place in ways she never expected or dared to hope. Already, she felt reborn.

'You on holiday?'

The unexpected voice startled her. A boy stood at her side, following her gaze out to sea. He was blonde, with summer-coloured skin, dressed in shorts and tee shirt.

'No,' she replied, looking away.

'Local then?'

When she didn't answer, the boy tried again.

'I'm William – Wim to my friends.'

When she still didn't reply, he sighed and walked away. 'Party on the beach tonight, eight o'clock,' he shouted from a little way off.

She watched him go. He was tall and broad shouldered. But it was the strands of breeze-tousled hair she noticed first, and the small winding tattoo on his ankle. As always, she focussed in on the little things, the seemingly insignificant.

The evening was still and unusually warm for the time of year. She sieved sand between her toes as she approached the small group of friends. One of the boys had brought a guitar and sat on driftwood noodling out a few chords. A small fire spat sea coal and smoked.

Wim spotted her between the dunes and smiled. He took her a beer. 'Glad you came.'

She noticed his eyes for the first time. They were a soft blue, like seagull eggs.

'I come here all the time,' she said.

He raised the bottle in her direction. 'Beer?'

She nodded, taking it. 'Cheers.'

'Would you like to join us? I could introduce you to everyone.'

She scanned the group. The boys were lean and tall like Wim, laughing and joking about. The girls, already young women, whispered confidences, casting furtive glances at the boys. One girl in particular was staring hard in their direction.

'No, thank you. Think I'll just walk for a while.'

'Want some company?'

'If you like.'

They followed the line of the dunes, away from the party, sipping beer and saying very little. He tried to make conversation but as they reached the shore, she stopped him.

'Listen.'

'To what?'

'Just listen and tell me what you hear.'

He mentioned the faint laughter from the party they'd left behind, the guitar thrumming in and out on the breeze, a distant car.

She shook her head and pointed to the horizon.

'What about the sea?'

'What about it?'

'Can't you hear it?'

He listened again, concentration furrowing his brow.

'I hear the waves lapping onto the sand.'

She sighed, showing her disappointment and noticed Wim blush.

'Well, what do *you* hear?

She pulled her dress over her head and walked into the surf. Twilight glistened, the sky at their backs now rimmed with ochre.

'Hey, be careful, the water's cold and the currents are strong here!'

She could hear the uncertainty and concern in Wim's voice but kept going and soon began to swim, a flowing rhythm that matched the ebb of the tide.

Wim pulled off his shirt and went in after her. Soon they were in deep and treading water.

She took his face in her hands. Her eyes were pleading.

'Listen!'

They heard their hearts pounding in their ears, the surf breaking against them, their breath coming in gasps. Their hair became streaked by the sunset. Wim shuddered.

'Who *are* you?'

She smiled and put her finger to his lips. Then she cupped her hands around his ears.

'Shhh. Slow down. Listen.'

He closed his eyes. Her touch awakened something in him. The air carried new sounds.

The sea, now a cymbal, brushed a rumba, Besame Mucho. A lone seabird ascended the strings of a Stradivarius. The wind whispered, *this is for you my children.*

Wim smiled. 'Now I hear.'

'Good. Let's go back.'

He looked disappointed, confused, as if not wanting the magic to end. She could feel it in the tingle of her spine.

They were cold as they stepped from the surf. Neither wished to speak, so lost were they in the song of the rolling sea. Their every sense enlivened.

The party fire was a warm oasis, the friends, ghostly silhouettes. These were the sounds and songs of youth, of hope. He found her hand in the darkness and meshed his fingers with hers.

'Are you ready to tell me your name yet?'

'Will my name change how you feel at this moment?'

'No.'

She looked back out to sea and he followed her gaze.

'Then let the song continue a little while longer.'

Silentworld

We thought the ice would be silent. We were wrong. It creaked and groaned like the bows of a storm-driven galleon. True silence, profound and absolute, could only be imagined. And yet I bear witness to such a silent world; I have been there and returned.

The Antarctic day began like any other in late summer, the wan light separating day from night in a well-rehearsed, half-hearted manner. There would be more ice cores to drill, more layers to investigate, more samples to take and more coffee to drink… much more.

We sat around the table in quiet contemplation of the coming day and ate breakfast. Chief Scientific Officer, Katie Burns had her laptop open already and tapped away distractedly as Tom packed up the equipment and Helen shrugged on her down jacket. She was always ready first. For my own part, I poured another coffee and lit a cigarette.

"Put that thing out," snapped Katie, still staring at her screen.

Wearily I complied. "Must we do this every morning?"

Katie looked up at me equally wearily. "Until you finally get it, yes." She returned her attention to the laptop. "We're investigating a new site today folks. The satellite images have highlighted a fault line that may prove interesting."

"What do we need?" asked Tom.

"We may eventually need to move the DISC drill, but for now, we just take a peek."

"Should I pack the hand augers?"

"Good idea Tom, we can take a few samples while we're there."

Katie snapped the laptop shut and shot me an order without another glance. "Get the transport ready, Mr Curry, on our way in fifteen."

Mr Curry, not Sam. It was Tom and it was Helen, but I was always Mr Curry. Never mind, it was just a job, and the pay was good for a couple of windy months of isolation. I could always put on the headphones, close my eyes and pretend I was alone. Maybe I was.

Loading sleds had been easy in the beginning, before the cold had reached my bones by way of deep cracks in my skin. Now I was all fingers and thumbs… but at least they were all still there. Helen came out to help me.

"You should keep the gloves on, Sam."

I gave her a rueful smile. "Can't work the straps with them on."

"Here, let me give you a hand."

She calls me Sam. That's nice. Helen is plain but kind-hearted, which I find attractive. There's nothing there of course… between us I mean… but at least she doesn't look down on me. We had the transport ready in ten.

The wind was less fierce today, so we made good progress. We soon arrived near the edge of a long crevasse, at least ten metres wide.

"Looks like we won't need the drill after all," remarked Helen.

"Providing it's safe," replied Tom. "Could be still moving."

"What do you think, Mr Curry?" asked Katie.

I was the safety man; even she had to defer to me on such matters. The project demanded deep ice exploration, but not at any cost. This was military sponsored research though, and that could change the dynamic.

"We should monitor the ice movement for a few days; see what we're dealing with here."

"This is the chance we've been waiting for," said Helen. "It could save months of drilling."

Helen was right, but it was extremely risky. "Or it could

set us back a year if we lose equipment or worse still..." I replied, leaving the thought hanging.

Katie, as always, was pragmatic. "Plant a few sensors, Tom. We can take a view in forty-eight hours."

As Tom did so, I walked to the edge of the crevasse to stare down into its depths. The sheer scale was mesmerising. I was looking back a million years, maybe two. Even I was willing to take a few risks to find out more.

I turned back towards the team, intending to say so, when the wind hit. It came without warning, an invisible force that slammed into us from nowhere. I watched the heavy packs lift from the sleds like paper kites as I was driven back towards the edge of the crevasse. I heard the panicked cries of the team and dug my heels in hard, but to little effect. I reached out my arms, desperate for something to cling to, but felt only wind driven ice. Everything seemed to slow down and I noticed Tom battling to free a coil of rope from one of the sleds. A few agonising moments later, I was over and airborne.

I accepted my impending death without fear or regret, but to my surprise, death did not come in the way I expected. My fall was long and felt like slow motion. I began to dream of home and childhood, of warm, safe hands. Strangely, there were also shadows lurking at the edge of my vision at which I dared not look too closely.

Then, inexplicably, I emerged into an enormous cavern, where the walls glittered with crystals. There was music in the air or perhaps more accurately, strange and complex sound. In the centre of this cavern was a sapphire blue lake and hovering above this water, an orb, like a small planet consisting only of ocean, flowing in graceful tides.

At the edge of the lake rested a small boat which I boarded without really understanding why. It immediately drifted towards the orb and I could see now that it was a sphere of about twenty metres across. If I was in fact still falling, I was completely unaware of it. My mind was so convinced by this very detailed vision it had become my new reality. On reaching the orb, I stretched out my hand into its waters and felt at once part of it, and so, without further hesitation I abandoned myself to this water world and plunged within.

The silence was absolute. No greater silence could I imagine. It was as though even my heart had ceased to function as this new world encompassed me, enveloped me in its womb. I swam with the currents that bore me ever onward and I felt as though I was metamorphosing in some way that I couldn't explain.

My thoughts returned once more to my childhood home and there before me it appeared, as real as once it was in every detail: the garden in which I played each summer, the marguerites by the red front door, the chestnut tree with the old swing secured to a spreading limb, and through the window, my father in his favourite chair, reading a newspaper.

As I drank in this vision, revelling in its nostalgic joy, those lurking shadows forced themselves upon me like storm-driven clouds and abruptly, it was gone. For a moment I mourned in darkness, but soon another picture materialized from the gloom. I saw myself as a young man, alone again in the University library, buried in books. Sadness gripped me until I thought I may be overwhelmed by it. As my soul grieved, a new light appeared before my eyes which drew me in like a moth to a flame. Within this light my senses exploded into a new kaleidoscopic vision. I became aware… of all life… all consciousness, as though it was part of my own. The universe and all its history opened up to my thoughts, with time no longer behaving as a linear thing. I *became* the universe. But it was too much to conceive, it almost crushed me. I focussed inward to find myself again and this silent world gently let me move on.

I tried to speak but my voice was lost and for the first time since my fall began, I remembered fear. The shadows re-appeared at the periphery of my sight, growing like dark septicaemic veins that crept ever closer. Then, I realised there were others sharing this silent world with me. Though I couldn't see them, I could sense their presence. There seemed to be a multitude, an impossible number.

More visions came to me; my own life and the lives of these others, the familiar and the strange. I could see other worlds through their eyes. I saw creatures that resembled seahorses living in vast underwater cities with crystal towers, living rocks that flowed like lava in great steaming lakes, and then elemental spirits that coalesced into immense, colourful clouds. And there was something else, something greater still within the silence that would not be revealed.

My journey continued. In the next moment I metamorphosed into something I could not fully understand. Even my thought patterns changed. I swam no longer in the silent world but in the depths of a great sea, teeming with fish of all descriptions. I swam with elegant efficiency and incredible speed amongst coral and rippling weed until suddenly I swept upwards, breaking the surface of the sea and taking to the sky like a great bird.

I soared ever upward, exhilarated by the freedom, higher and higher into the blue; twisting, turning, diving. And then… I returned once again to my own familiar self, and it was as though I was now expected to choose my path. And so, I chose.

When I entered the hut at the research station, no one seemed surprised to see me. The team sat eating breakfast and preparing for the new day as always.

"Ready the transport, Mr Curry," said Katie Burns, "on our way in fifteen."

Ray

"I could have taken Joe Louis at forty," he brags, and I believe him. The days we spent side by side, with hammers or saws in hand, have left me with little doubt as to Ray's former power, both in arm and in thought. I lift him from the bed and his weight is now inconsequential, though he marvels at my ability to do so. He must use the toilet and I fear his ebullient praise of my efforts masks the shame he feels.

There is little dignity to be had in such a slow deterioration, robbed of hope. And yet love, as is so often the case, lends solidarity if not grace to this inevitable reduction. The days of physical strength now reside in memories, but the gentle humour still bubbles to the surface, revealing the true strength of the man.

We've known each other for about fifteen years. Not long really, but enough time to build understanding and respect, and to love; though the word is never spoken. And now, as the blood thickens to sludge within his veins, his stricken wife and daughter minister to his needs as I lift, and share a little joke to ease the tension.

He has come to our home for his last days, to the spare room, into a bed with the wooden cot he made for his granddaughter residing beneath it; unused for twelve years or so but kept folded away, ready for the next generation. The unintended symbolism flips my stomach.

The women are in charge. They never complain nor shrink from any task. There's food and drink to administer, medication, bedsores to relieve, endless cleaning, and comfort to bring in soft words or gentle touch. Their hearts would break later. For now, while life remains, they will not indulge in sorrow, but rather in service to one whom they have loved and love still. I am on the fringe, uncertain

73

how to help. I get on with life, work and play, convincing myself there would plenty of time for goodbyes, not really grasping what is required of me or when.

So I think about his life, the things he has told me about growing up in Morpeth, Northumberland; the poverty that made him a socialist, the time in the Navy that inspired him to seek a better life in Australia, and the homesickness that brought him back like a migrating bird. It has been a full and interesting life, and one that I have glimpsed on occasions, listening like a fascinated child to his many stories. I am a better man thanks to Ray and his subtle guidance.

Awkwardly, I thank him for everything he has done for us. I should be thanking him for who he is, or has been, rather than this, but I can hardly frame a sentence.

'I did what I had to do,' he replies, and shrugs. I just nod. I don't say any of the things I should say, not now anyway, not until I'm on my own, speaking to the air.

The doctor comes but no priest. He won't have a priest attend, though his Catholic sister wishes it. He has long since turned his back on the church of his childhood. He is content for me to believe in God, but World War II finally expunged any lingering faith that hadn't already been beaten out of him by overzealous church school teachers.

'When you've seen your mates blown to bits before your eyes...' he would say, without giving further voice to the thought. So, the doctor talks to him of where he might be heading once the curtains close. I'm not privy to that conversation, but he seems content enough with the outcome.

Ray pulls me close and gently refers to his wife of many years. "Pat... she's going to need looking after," he states rather than asks.

"Don't worry yourself about that," I reply, "you have my word."

74

He nods his approval and we share a silent moment. I feel guilty because I know it will be his daughter and not I who will shoulder most of that responsibility.

He has to be on a trolley now, at the foot of the bed. His eyes are closed and his breath comes in shallow, ragged gasps. He has shrunk so much, his dentures no longer fit and they have had to be removed. The women have left momentarily and I am alone with him. I place my hand on his forehead and say simply, 'I hope you're comfortable, Ray,' unsure as to whether he can still hear me.

He takes a few more breaths, and then stops. I know he is gone. It was as though those few words were all he needed to finally let go. I linger a few seconds longer, afraid of what comes next. I leave the room and meet my wife on the landing, the daughter who worshipped him like a god. 'I think he's gone,' I say, and see shock and pain as though it was unexpected.

I must tell my daughter now, the granddaughter for whom he made, with skilled hands, a walking stick, so they could be "the same" on their strolls to the creek. The granddaughter he fashioned the little toy shop for and the puppet theatre, the doll's house replica of our home. She crumples before me like laundry. 'No, not *my* Grandad,' she pleads.

I take over now. I have a purpose. No one else can make the funeral arrangements, only me. I can bury my grief for now and do this last thing for Ray. The service will be at my current church, the URC and the Catholic family won't come. The divide between heaven and earth is not as great as that between the faiths it would seem. But I will not betray his wishes, and I will pray for him and ask God to welcome such a man as this into his loving arms.

It is his daughter's wish that we plant a tree in the corner of our garden and place him there, two oaks sharing the same soil. It is a splendid tree, straight and strong, and will most likely outlive everyone who knew him.

We must wait before talking about the joyful times spent together, until grief matures into something manageable. But until then we have this tree, and perhaps one day, a hundred years from now, it will be cut down and the wood used by some skilled craftsman not yet born, to make a walking stick for his granddaughter, or a crib in which to lay his own child. And in that dream I find the beauty of it all, the wonder in this never-ending story. For now, as winter chill brings these oaks to slumber, we will lay down our flowers there and remember Ray.

Like a Thief in the Night

These days, Ethel likes to sit in her bay window watching the street. She used to worry about who could see her and preferred to hide behind the translucent safety of net curtains. Now, she couldn't care less. The garden which separates her from the street is small and simple, framed by a low brick wall and a blue-painted wooden gate. The tiny lawn is neat and the borders sparse but free of weeds. Curtains drawn aside and spectacles in place, she can see most of the goings on along Union Road, at least as far as the chemist.

On an ordinary day like today, all kinds of people could walk by; the steady stream of kids going to school, the odd hooded youth with head bowed and hands in pockets, the window cleaner who turned up once a fortnight, and usually a couple of new mums with babies in pushchairs, heading for the coffee shop or doctors surgery around the corner.

Today, Ethel noticed, number 9 was having what looked like a new fridge delivered and the delivery men were unloading the large box from their van with well-practiced ease. It made Ethel think of Frank. Frank had been a strong man, but gentle with it. *A good husband he was... cut off in his prime.*

She glances at a framed photograph on the sideboard which shows Ethel and a tall dark Frank on holiday somewhere years ago, and blows it a kiss. Her eyes turn bleary for a moment, so she cleans her glasses on her cardigan and waits for them to clear.

The box is going in through the front door now. *Mrs Brady seems to get a lot of deliveries,* thinks Ethel, *I wonder if I should order something? The microwave spat sparks yesterday... maybe it's time to get a new one.*

The sun suddenly breaks free of the clouds and bathes

the street in honeyed light. Ethel smiles, her thoughts as warm as the view. *How wonderful everything looks in the sunshine, even number 12 with its wonky satellite dish and drab pebbledash.* She closes her eyes and remembers a faraway holiday, where the sunshine never stopped, the drinks flowed and the sea glistened as though in a fairy tale. She bathes in the memory of it, and feels anew the spark of youth, though lost, never forgotten.

A small and raucous motorbike fizzes by, ruffling her daydreams. *That would be young Alex from number 24 again,* she thinks. *If only he didn't make so much noise he would be a decent lad. Out of work though, like most of the youngsters around here. Where's the hope?*

She spots a cobweb, filling the handle of the blue Wedgwood vase sat on the windowsill to her left, tuts and takes out a hankie from her cardigan pocket to deal with it. *Mother gave me that vase, well, gave it to me and Frank back in the day… can't be having cobwebs on it.* 'Can you see me Mother?' she says out loud, 'sat here cleaning your vase? I'm being a good girl, just like you said I should.' Then, a familiar noise grabs her attention… a click of the sneck on the garden gate.

That's odd, she thinks, *who could that be?* A man is already through the gate and heading for Ethel's front door. He is middle-aged, grey haired and dressed in a dark suit. Another similar man joins him. The first man notices Ethel through the window and smiles. 'Hello,' he mouths and points at the door. Ethel just looks at him as though he were mad. He furrows his brow, fumbles in his briefcase and brings out a copy of *The Watchtower*, which he shows to Ethel with a hopeful look on his face. Ethel continues to stare at him blankly. The men glance at each other, shrug and leave. *Twits,* thinks Ethel as they disappear down the street.

78

The delivery van is leaving now and the driver catches Ethel's attention. He is wearing a T-shirt and his arms are heavily tattooed. *Wouldn't get past my step with arms like that, bloody gypsy, eh Frank?* The van drives away and Ethel resumes her watch with a dismissive sniff.

Her eyes are getting heavy. The chair is a comfy one and the room is warm. She leans back and starts daydreaming again. *If only we'd had kids*, she thinks. There'd nearly been one... once... God's will, Frank had said, but she'd never been able to get her head around that one. *Never mind, no point in regrets, not now... too much water under the bridge.*

Ethel realises she must have fallen asleep because the kids are coming back home from school now, in their usual happy, noisy way. She smiles and waves and some of them wave back. *What must they think of me sat here in the same place every day?* She feels a now familiar flutter in her chest which makes her cough. *Time for a cuppa*, she thinks and gets up slowly, taking time to straighten her back. Her legs ache and she grimaces as she walks into the kitchen to put the kettle on.

Everything is clean and in its place, the way Mother had taught her. She puts the gas on and absentmindedly fills the kettle. She's looking out of the back window now, at Frank's shed. 'Kettle's on, Frank,' she whispers.

Ethel likes her tea strong and says the same thing every time. 'Just like my men,' she giggles, absentmindedly. She pours boiling water onto the Rington's teabag in her best mug and leaves it to brew. Colour first, *then* flavour, the man had said. She liked it when the Rington's man came and always bought something, whether she needed it or not. But that's on a Thursday and today is... what's today again? She opens the pantry and checks the calendar which had been stuck on the back of the door. Tuesday, today is

Tuesday, she thinks and crosses it off… or did I cross it off at breakfast? She shrugs and goes back to the tea which is now a pleasing dark brown. That'll do, she thinks and splashes the milk in.

Ethel resumes her seat at the window a little out of breath and immediately notices a pair of crows going into the chimney at number 7. The nets had blown off in last week's storm and she'd known what would happen soon after. They'll have bother with that, she thinks. Frank would have been straight over to tell them but I'm blowed if I'm going out… not with my feet.

She glances at the clock on the mantelpiece. 'Nearly time for the soaps,' she says. '*Union Road* will have to manage without me for a while… now where's that remote?' She gets up again, rummages down the side of the sofa and with a look of triumph finds it. 'Can't hide from me for long!'

It's then she sees him, as she turns around to click on the TV, sat in his armchair by the fire, as bold as brass. She nearly drops her tea in fright. 'Frank?' she warbles, 'Frank?'

'Yes lass, it's only me, don't worry yerself.'

'What you doin' back?' she quips. 'Hell too hot for you then?'

Frank laughs. 'You could say that, but I wouldn't know. I've come to get you lass, you ready?'

'Yes Frank, I'm ready, more than ready.'

'Right then lass, get back in yer seat and put that tea on the sill before you make a mess.'

'Yes Frank, I will.'

Ethel sits, puts her head back, looks across at Frank and smiles. 'What a fright you gave me,' she says, 'coming in here like a thief in the night.'

Frank smiles back warmly. He looks just like he did on

their wedding day, all rugged and handsome. The sun is shining again and the room lights up, all aglow. Strangely, the sounds of the street are gone and all she hears now is her own slow breathing.

'You're a fine man Frank,' she whispers, 'a fine man indeed.'

Her eyes grow heavy once more, her heart flutters like a moth in a lampshade and though she is uncertain and a little afraid, she feels a hand take hers and smiles.

Time to go lass, echoes softly in her mind as she drifts away into the most wonderful… restful… sleep.

Isobel

It was during the first age of magic, a time veiled in shadow, when those who are now called witches or wizards emerged from the forests and caves of the higher hills as a people of great renown, considered wise and blessed by the gods. Many rulers, even mighty Kings, would consult these wise folk before battle to foresee their future or to ask for intercession on their behalf with the gods. They would offer great riches in return for victory or at the least some advantage over their enemies.

Such people were tuned to the Earth and its many rhythms, mastering the power to heal, and yes, destroy if necessary. They were loved and feared in equal measure, possessed of the sight and a deep, old knowledge, passed down from the time of the first Lords of the Earth, named The Fathers of the Beginning.

It is said, by those who protect the old ways, that the greatest of these was born to a princess, the only daughter of a strong but ruthless King who ruled a land in the east, and fathered by a First Lord named by some as Yeqon, a fallen angel of heaven.

The child was a girl and thought to be a goddess, with all the secret powers of nature at her command. She had control over birth, life, and death. She became known as the Goddess of the Dark of the Moon or the Nameless One, who could command even the demons of the underworld.

Her strength and beauty were much admired and she had many suitors amongst Earths greatest heroes, who were considered a race of demigods themselves and given the name Nephilim.

Thus a great and noble lineage had begun and though, down the many centuries, such great power was inevitably diluted through each passing generation, the old knowledge was protected and nurtured within every firstborn daughter.

One such daughter was born Isobel Collins at a time when the world was a very dark and dangerous place. Plague and famine robbed the people of hope and the land seemed perpetually gripped in the steely fist of winter. Desperation led to many dark and terrible deeds and with every new evil came the winnowing canker that is fear and suspicion.

Despite their illustrious heritage, Isobel's family, like most around them, was poor, daily striving to make a living from the harsh landscape. But whilst other people's crops failed, succumbing to frozen soil set as hard as iron, theirs did not. And though all around, domestic animals died for want of enough feed and warmth, theirs did not. Isobel and her mother saw to that, drawing on all the skills and intuition passed faithfully down to them and practiced long, since early childhood. Though not thriving, they survived, whilst their neighbours faltered and died, succumbing to hunger and disease. They kept themselves apart, trying to stave off the inevitable day of reckoning.

As time passed, grinding poverty and sickness led people, with much encouragement from the church it has to be said, to blame the Devil and his demons for their plight and inevitably suspicion along with jealous eyes fell upon the Collins family and their unnatural good fortune.

A meeting was convened of the remaining town's folk in the great hall, the theme of which was tragically to become common in the years that followed and devastating to anyone considered in any way "different". Picture now the scene...

A large broad-shouldered man sits at the head of the hall on an ornately carved wooden throne chair. His long brown beard is tinged with grey and his deep set hazel eyes stare long and hard at the ragtag bunch of people sat on benches before him. At his side is a priest, a stranger to the town, an emissary of the Pope.

The women are gaunt and weary, the children sullen and silent but the men still manage a look of defiance that belies their ruined circumstances.

'We are cursed!' shouts one man, whose sunken face gives him the look of a crazed skull.

'Aye, cursed!' shouts another. 'Disease and hunger stalk our homes. Our fingers bleed but our toil is fruitless. God has abandoned us!'

'Aye!' say the crowd in unison.

The priest steps forward and raises his hand. The people quieten immediately but he pauses for effect, looking at them. He is a striking man with a sharp nose and high forehead. He stands straight and imposing, calm but intense.

'Not everyone is… *cursed,* we have heard,' he says, emphasising the word "cursed".

No one replies.

'Well?' he continues, 'have we heard wrong?'

A woman who is sat to one side stands up. Her clothes are rags and her hair a tangled thicket of brown curls.

'The Collins, sir, the family at the edge of the wood, they alone escape this torment,' she mutters.

'They alone?' asks the priest, feigning astonishment.

'Yes sir.'

'Curious. And why, do you think, God in His great mercy and infinite wisdom should smile upon them alone?'

'I know not, sir,' she replies and sits down quickly.

The priest turns to address the assembly once again. 'And why is this fortunate family not amongst us all here today?'

'They keeps themselves to themselves,' says a short squat man on the front row.

'Do they now?' replies the priest. 'And have they shared any of this good fortune with you?'

No one speaks out, but many shake their heads and cast their eyes upon the floor.

'I see,' says the priest, 'and what, may I ask, have you done about it?'

No one dares answer. Eventually, the man sat on the throne chair speaks up for the first time.

'Nothing,' he rasps. 'They are afraid.'

The priest turns his attention to the man, feigning confusion.

'Afraid? What might they be afraid of, Luther? What can be more frightening than this great suffering I see before me?'

Luther pauses. 'Magic,' he replies, 'the earth lore of the old gods.'

'There is but one God!' snaps the priest, 'but there are many demons. If this were God's work then all this land would be so blessed... would it not?'

He turns to face the assembly again. 'The fact that you, by your own testimony are cursed, your very hands cursed, your land cursed and yet they, *they* alone are not? This can only be the work of Satan!'

'Our babies are stillborn!' sobs a woman from the back of the hall.

'Aye, and our water poisoned,' growls another.

Soon the whole room is in uproar, with shouts and accusations echoing from every wall and rafter. Eventually the priest raises his hands again and gradually, order is restored.

'Who will bring them here?' he asks.

No one responds, fear once again reestablishing its thorny grip. Then from the shadows a swarthy man steps forward. He is dressed in black leather and a long winding scar adorns his face and neck. He wears a thin curved knife at his belt and another in his boot. His eyes are rimmed with charcoal and on his left hand a silver ring shines hypnotically in the lamplight.

'My name is Hassan i Sabbah,' he growls, in a thick accent, 'and I fear no one, not even the Devil himself.'

None of the assembled recognises Hassan nor had they even noticed him until that moment. Luther stands quickly, a look of puzzlement on his face. The room fills with confusion and doubt.

'Why are you here? Where did you come from?' demands Luther.

Hassan smiles and folds his arms. 'The village was quiet and I saw light at the window... I was curious,' he replies casually, 'but how fortunate for you that I happened by. I will fetch the witch and bring her before you.'

'We have not used the term witch,' says the priest, 'but I suppose we were getting there. Why are you prepared to do God's work, stranger?'

'I care not for your God,' replies Hassan. 'I ask only this: if a witch there proves to be in this town then she becomes my property. I will take her away from here and she will never trouble you again.'

If a witch she proves to be then she will burn, thinks the priest, *but I need not be truthful with this heathen.* 'What say you, Luther?' he asks.

Luther walks up to Hassan and studies his face. He is a head taller than the stranger and much stronger in body. He gauges that should there be any trouble he could put the man in his place comfortably enough. He eyes the stranger's knife before answering.

'We take care of our own business,' he growls in a low rumble.

Hassan smiles again, unmoved by the rebuttal.

86

'I am curious, what need do you have of a witch, stranger?' asks the priest.

Hassan regards the priest warily.

'I serve not my own needs, but those of my master. I have travelled the length and breadth of this land to find a true sister of the old religion. Many have I seen but few have I yet approved.'

'Who is your master and what does he require of a witch? Is he also in league with the powers of hell?' asks the priest, his voice now hoarse from overuse.

Hassan laughs humourlessly. 'My master is not a man, priest, nor evil. Perhaps I should have said "mistress" though the term is confusing. I should have your tongue for such insolence, though in the merciful name of Princess Persepolis I will stay my hand and forgive your ignorance this time.'

Luther bristles at the remark. 'I will fetch the Collins here myself. They will have the chance to answer their accusers. We are getting ahead of ourselves.'

Hassan bows and steps back into the shadows.

'Who will come with me?' asks Luther.

'I will,' says the short, wide man on the front bench.

'Thank you, Robert.' Luther slaps the man on the shoulder. 'Let us go then, and the rest of you can await our return here.'

'I will come too,' says the priest, with a look that brooks no argument.

'Very well,' replies Luther, 'bring a lamp and lead the way.'

They look around for Hassan but he is gone. Luther, Robert and the priest set off into the gloom of the night, through the centre of the village, down past the church to the river, across the old bridge and along the track that leads to the Collins' farm, at the edge of the wood.

They soon arrive at the clearing occupied by the

farmhouse and are surprised to see Harry Collins, Isobel's father and David his son waiting for them outside the front door. Both have swords in their hands.

How did they know? is Luther's first thought.

'I know why you're here,' calls out Harry. 'I wondered how long it would take.'

'Don't be a fool, Harry,' urges Luther, 'we need to bring you all to council. There's questions to answer that's all, no need for violence.'

Harry spits. 'I know what you think. No one is going near my family, not unless it is over my dead body.'

The priest steps forward with the lamp, illuminating the scene in a sallow, golden hue.

'We are here on the Lord's work, Mr Collins, and Satan cannot stand against us, so why do you suppose that *you* are able? Now step aside.'

Suddenly David Collins lunges forward, stabbing the priest in the arm. The injured priest screams and Luther looks poised to retaliate, but Harry's sword leaps to his throat, stopping just short of drawing blood.

'Think about this, Harry,' says Robert. 'You can't fight the whole town.'

To Robert's surprise, Harry smiles. 'Maybe not, but without Luther and his priest, will they come?'

Robert had no answer for that. They probably wouldn't.

'If not the townsfolk then the militia,' rasps the priest.

'Miles away,' replies Harry, scornfully, 'and who's gonna call them when yur gone, worm?'

The door to the farmhouse suddenly opens and a young girl of about fifteen years steps out. She is tall and slim with thick red hair, plaited and curled up on top of her head. In the weak light she shines like the moon.

'Get back inside Isobel!' snaps Harry, clearly unnerved by her sudden appearance.

88

'No father,' she replies, 'this is not the way. We knew this day would come and now we must face it.'

'Isobel, you don't understand. You are too young. These fools would kill us all,' says Harry, a note of desperation colouring his voice.

'Isobel is right Harry.'

Isobel's mother joins them now and puts her hand lightly on Harry's shoulder. 'We can't fight everyone my love. Better to share our lore and let the people decide our fate. They are good people, they will understand.'

'They are superstitious fools, Eleanor! They understand nothing.'

'You will all get a fair hearing,' says Luther, 'I give you my word of honour.'

Harry spits again in disgust. 'We have no reason to trust you and even less to trust this priest. I say we kill you now and take the consequences. If we die, we die fighting.'

Then out of the shadows a blur and a breeze sweeps amongst them. In the blink of an eye, Harry and David are no longer holding their swords. They stand bemused and suddenly very vulnerable.

'What trickery is this?' Harry exclaims, holding up his empty hands.

Hassan confronts them, with both swords pointing back at their chests.

'Who the hell are you?' asks Harry.

'Either your best friend or worst nightmare, you decide.'

'Let this stop now!' shouts Eleanor, taking charge. 'We will come with you peacefully. There is no need for bloodshed this night.'

'Very well,' says Luther, 'let us return to the meeting place.'

The priest seethes, holding his arm tightly with his

anger barely in check. Blood leaks through his fingers, warm and sticky.

'Let me first bandage your arm, priest,' says Eleanor, aware of his distress.

'Do not touch me!' he snaps back, angrily.

She shrugs, clearly saddened. 'As you wish. Let us go.'

'I pray that you are right about this, Eleanor,' says Harry, 'but I fear the worst.'

They trudge silently back to the great hall, each alone in their thoughts. The town is quiet and gloomy, without even any sign of cats or dogs, most of which have long since provided much needed sustenance during the hard winter. As they cross the river, the cloying stench of sewage turns their stomachs, and now amongst the narrow streets the familiar stink of death and decay, the ever-present consequence of disease. The great hall is now a beacon in the near distance, light leaking from every window and crack in the walls.

They enter to a full house, every seat and corner taken. The few babies present cry weakly but other than that, the people are quiet, pensive, waiting apprehensively for proceedings to begin. Luther leads the party to the front of the hall. Hassan, who had silently brought up the rear, once again melts away into the night.

'So, here we are,' says Luther. 'Let us begin in earnest and come straight to the point. Of what do we accuse these people?'

Silence. The air seems compressed.

'Speak now or forever hold your peace,' he demands.

A tall man steps forward. He is sunken-cheeked like the rest but stands straight and proud. 'I can speak for those who tend this land,' he says with some authority.

'Very well, Ethan,' replies Luther. 'Go on, we are listening.'

'I have farmed here all me life,' he begins, 'and so did me father and his father before 'im. There's been hard winters aplenty, and many lean times. But never, *never* before has the soil refused to feed us, nor have our beasts withered and died in field or barn!'

'Aye!' shouts a group of men, who gather nearby as he continues to speak.

'And yet, these people, these Collins who came amongst us not more than three years ago, can still milk goat and cow and take provision from the earth.'

'Aye!' the cry goes up again, this time from more of the assembly.

'By what skill do they succeed where we fail?' asks someone from the back, and then abruptly everyone seems to be shouting at the same time.

'We die from hunger and sickness while these people thrive!'

'They have cursed us!'

The priest finally lifts his good arm appealing for quiet. He looks pale and weak now and so it takes Luther to finally restore calm. 'Quiet now! Quiet!' he roars and finally the people settle down again, reduced to mutterings.

'There is no God-given skill at work here,' claims the priest. 'There is only witchcraft. I feel it with every fibre of my being.'

'Listen to me, good people!' shouts Eleanor suddenly. 'I can understand your pain. You are hungry and desperate. But do not look for evil here. The only evil is ignorance. It is true we have knowledge, old wisdom that helps us to keep our animals alive, to stave off sickness. And we are willing to share this with you if you will accept it.'

'So!' growls the priest. 'From her own mouth you have heard it! Such *old* knowledge as she calls it, pagan lore, is a gift from Satan to his servants on earth. We are not as ignorant as you might suppose… witch!'

'NO!' Isobel calls out, her voice shrill and piercing. 'We are good people, a kind and loving family. We can show you our ways. We can help you.'

'Get ye behind me Satan!' roars the priest. 'We are God's people. Your ways are not our ways.'

'Their so-called ways killed my child,' says a young woman to one side. Eleanor immediately recognises the girl and closes her eyes, inwardly dreading what she knows will come next.

'Step forward, Sarah. Don't be afraid,' says Luther, gently. 'Explain to us what you mean by that.' Sarah shuffles towards the front of the hall looking at her feet.

'My baby wouldn't stop crying,' she almost whispers.

'Speak up girl, so we can all hear,' says the priest, unsympathetic to her trembling uncertainty.

'My child, sir, she ailed day and night' she manages, a little louder. 'My mother thought she would be right eventually, with warm milk and honey, but she was hot, sir, and I was worried. I'd heard people talk down the market. They said that Mrs Collins had medicine, strong medicine, sir, that could help with fever. My mother said I shouldn't but I did, sir, I went to see Mrs Collins and took the babe with me.' Sarah hesitates and brings her palms to her face. A sob twitches her shoulders.

'You must go on, Sarah,' says Luther, as gently as possible.

'They took me in, sir,' she continues, 'and placed my little one on the table. The young one, Isobel, she was sent to gather weeds from the garden and from what she brought, they made a foul-smelling broth. They made my baby drink it, sir, and raised smoke from an oil burner that filled the room.'

'Witchcraft!' shouts the priest. 'Is it not just as I have said?'

'Aye!' choruses the assembly.

'Wait!' snaps Luther, staring long and hard at the priest. 'Let Sarah finish and Mrs Collins answer. We will have this done properly! Now, please go on Sarah.'

'I panicked, sir, couldn't help it. I was afraid. I grabbed my child and ran home fast as I could. The little one seemed to rally and for a while there was hope in my heart. But the next morning… she lay still and quiet in the crib… she was gone, sir… before I'd even named her.' Sarah breaks down, weeping into her hands and for a few moments that is the only sound in the hall.

'What say you about this, Mrs Collins?' asks Luther.

'The child was close to death when she came to us. Had she remained in our care she may just have had a chance, but…' Eleanor shrugs her shoulders.

'Liar!' screams Sarah, sobbing louder than ever.

Then the priest is on his feet again, and this time more controlled.

'What more evidence do you need?' he chimes calmly. 'They prosper while you and your families suffer and die. Your babies are stillborn or poisoned. Must you wait until the Devil himself walks into town?'

'What must we do then?' asks Ethan, the tall farmer.

'The Lord himself tells us what to do in Exodus, Chapter 22, Verse 18,' replies the priest. '*Thou shalt not suffer a witch to live!*'

Young David Collins, who had remained sullen and silent since stabbing the priest in the arm, is suddenly reenergised and throws himself at the priest in fury. He grasps the man by the throat and begins choking the life out of him.

'David no!' pleads Eleanor, but Harry takes his son's

lead and barrels into Luther, throwing him off his feet. They grapple on the floor, trading thunderous blows, as the priest's face turns red and then purple.

For a minute or so, it looks as though they might get the upper hand, but then the men of the town leap as one to their leader's defense and soon after, both Harry and David are pinned to the ground, helpless. The priest gasps for air, unable to speak, but Luther quickly regains his composure.

'I've seen and heard enough,' he says, emphatically. 'What say you all, innocent or guilty?'

'Guilty!' cries the whole assembly, rushing forward to grab Isobel and her mother.

But before they can do so, Eleanor raises her hands out in front of her, causing a shockwave of air to arc out towards the crowd. It hits them like a tidal wave, throwing them to the floor like ragdolls.

'Go, quickly,' she commands Isobel. 'Protect the line, for you are the one now. Go before my strength fails me!'

'Fire!' croaks the priest. 'Luther, they fear the flame.'

Luther grabs a flaming torch from the wall and advances warily towards Eleanor and Isobel. Eleanor blows at the torch as though it were a candle, causing a fierce wind to engulf Luther. The flame singes his hair and beard and then gutters, almost dying in a cloud of smoke and soot. But it does not extinguish entirely. As the wind begins to falter, so the flame springs back to life.

'Isobel,' says her mother softly, 'the things we spoke of have now come to pass. Goodbye, my daughter.'

Isobel is filled with sorrow and weeps for her family but knows that she must escape to protect the old religion, her sacred cause. She flees towards the door and in the confusion makes it out into the moonless night. She runs and runs, soon reaching the town gate, where a thunderous roar stops her in her tracks. She turns, watching in horror, as the great hall explodes into a ball of flame, shooting sparks high into the ink black sky. The sight is paralysing, rooting her to the spot, as the flames cauterise her soul.

'You cannot remain here.'

The voice seems to come from the town wall itself. Isobel strains her eyes but there is only darkness, shadow and cold stone.

'Who is there? Reveal yourself!'

A figure in black flows out from obsidian depths like a ghost. 'Hassan i Sabbah, at your service.'

'That name I *will* remember, Hassan i Sabbah.' she replies, bitterly. 'A demon now stands before me.'

'I am here to help you fulfil your destiny, Isobel,' he purrs, in the accent of the merchants of cloth and spices. 'Come with me now and I will show you the wonders of the East. You could be like a princess in a new land.'

Isobel looks at the heavy town gate. It is locked and to get beyond that hurdle would be difficult enough. And then, a young girl alone and on the run may not last long in the open, even with her particular skills. *Maybe this Hassan is necessary now*, she thinks, *but one day, I will have my revenge.*

'Why should I trust you?'

'Because you have little choice and because you are of great value to someone I have sworn to serve.'

Isobel responds fiercely, stepping close to Hassan, snarling into his face. 'I am not an object to be traded, and should you wish to try, you will find to your cost that I am not easy to kill. And furthermore, Hassan i Sabbah, should you betray me, I will send a blight upon you and your master that people will forever speak of in awe!'

Hassan laughs. 'Of that I am certain, Isobel, but may we continue this discussion upon the road? Come with me now, before it is too late.'

Voices could be heard in the distance, a rising cacophony of trouble.

'Very well,' she replies, now resigned to her fate. 'What is your plan?'

Hassan takes Isobel by the hand and leads her to the wall on the east side of the gate tower. At first it seems as though there is nothing to see but stone and rock, but then she notices an iron grate which has been moved to one side.

'Here is the way but it is sheer and treacherous. It leads to the river on the north side where I have left my boat. You will have to hold onto me with all your strength and we may have need of your skill, but I believe we can make it. Climb onto my back if you will.'

The sound of horses' hooves joins the tumult of voices along with the crashing of the great hall as it burns noisily to the ground.

'Let us go then,' she says, and moving like a panther, Hassan obeys…

Even Pain

Solomon and Eve lay together, breathing the same air.

'I'm going to die soon,' said Solomon.

'I know,' replied Eve, her eyes no longer windows.

'Sorry,' he said.

'Sorry?'

'Yes. This is going to be harder for you than it is for me.'

Eve pressed closer to him. They were naked and the feel of him almost broke her.

'Shall I come with you?'

He smiled. 'I don't know where I'm going.'

'I've had words,' she said, eyes flicking upwards.

'Oh. You have, have you?'

'Yes. And she always listens to me.'

'She?'

Eve grinned mischievously. 'You heard.'

Solomon tried to laugh but it came out more like a wheeze. He felt something change. Inside.

'Kiss me,' he said, and she did. Eve licked his dry lips and then gently pressed. She trembled, wrung out by emotion.

When she separated from him, he was gone. She'd felt him go, but hung on, silently saying goodbye.

He was right; this would be harder for her. *This is life,* she thought, *right here, right now. This is what it really means; this is where it all leads.*

Out on the street, everything seemed so different; the sounds, the smells. No one knew. How could they? Eve looked up and wept. *Where are you?*

She spied a bird, circling high in the sky. *Sentimental fool,* she thought, but smiled and tasted the saltiness of her tears. *No, I was wrong; this is life, feeling things, even pain.*

Beyond the Awakening

Philip turned 136 today and was starting to feel his age. It wasn't a physical thing; most of those wrinkles had been engineered out years ago. Neither was it any sort of mental deficiency, he was easily smart enough to get by. No, it was more like the weariness of spirit that came with hanging around for too long without a purpose. In theory, you were allowed to live to the level of your intelligence quotient, in Philip's case 150, but many people have found that after about 130 years, enough is enough. There are exceptions of course. There are those who choose to see how far they can push it and it is rumoured that 300 is achievable, although this is widely disputed. Some of the more capable scientists will work on to around 200, but they are few and far between.

However, on his 136th birthday, Philip was pleased to find himself in the company of his great, great granddaughter Florence Rose. They sat together watching holographic cartoon characters sing *Happy Birthday to You* from the i-card she'd brought him, and it always gave him pleasure to see her so content.

When the song was over, Florence kissed his cheek and said, 'Tell me about the olden days, 3G.' This was her name for him, 3G, and it served them well enough.

'But I've told you before,' he pretended to complain.

'Then tell me again,' she insisted, settling into the crook of his arm.

Normally, Philip would simply begin by telling Florence about motorcars that used crude fuels to make them go, filling the air with smelly fumes, or how people had to go to work in factories every day to earn enough money for food and clothing. These things always amazed Florence. But today was different. It may just have been the mood he was in or perhaps recognition of the fact that, at ten years old, Florence was starting to understand the world around her far more. Kids were smarter these days, now that retinal streaming was compulsory from the age of six. He decided to go darker.

'You know, my darling, at one time, not so very long ago, people used to blow each other up with bombs, just because they didn't agree with one another.'

Florence went quiet for a few seconds. 'What kind of people, 3G?'

'Oh, any kind actually. Before the Awakening, one country could easily hate another or even groups of people within the same country who found they had different ideas about how the world should work. There were those who tried to work things out by talking and doing deals, but there were others who thought it was better to just hurt folk, beat the enemy into submission with force.'

Philip knew that Florence's mother wouldn't take kindly to him talking this way, but he felt a duty. She certainly wouldn't get this sort of history lesson from school.

'But why did they do such terrible things, 3G?'

'Oh, for money, power, all about greed mainly. But sometimes just to impose their own particular ideas on everyone else.'

Florence sighed and snuggled deeper into his arm. 'I'm glad the world is different now.'

Philip thought about that simple statement. In a lot of ways the world *was* a better place since the Awakening. There were no longer any global conflicts and those that still exhibited a trend towards the old ways were quickly reconditioned. Bio-food synthesis had all but eradicated hunger and sophisticated gene therapy techniques had long since provided health and well-being beyond the wildest dreams of his forefathers.

But, as far as he was concerned, by the time you reached the age of 136, certain nagging doubts began to surface. He'd wondered for some time about the mysterious "Fathers of the Beginning", the revered instigators of the Awakening. No one he knew had ever seen them or had any idea who they were. Equally, no one seemed to care about such things. It was enough for most citizens that the world didn't require anything of them but their minds. The entire population of the globe had been refocussed on discovery, research and innovation. New inventions appeared almost every day, and general understanding of the universe was almost absolute... almost.

'There were *some* good things about the olden days, Florence.'

'What were they?'

'Well, we didn't all have to believe the same thing for a start. We could make our own minds up about things.'

'What things?'

Philip hesitated. He wasn't really sure. 'Well, we could choose whether to eat meat or vegetables for a start. And there was no such thing as a synthburger either.'

Florence made a sick noise. 'You didn't eat animals did you, 3G? That's disgusting!'

Just then Florence's mother appeared at the door. 'What are you up to now? Not more gruesome tales of the old days I hope?'

Florence was theatrically pretending to vomit. '3G used to eat animals!'

Philip shifted uncomfortably in his seat. 'Well, that was a long time ago. Times have changed.'

'I've told you before about this,' scolded Florence's mother. She shook her head, exasperated.

'The girl needs to know her history!'

'Nothing before the Awakening has much relevance to

Florence; it's the future that's important. I will forgive you this once, as it's your birthday. I've brought you something.'

Softening, she smiled and handed him a rectangular parcel which he opened immediately. It was a framed £20 note behind glass. 'Joe got it from a guy he knows at the university. He reckons it's the genuine article, circa 2017.'

Philip stared at the note without saying anything for a little too long.

'Don't you like it, Pa?'

'Oh, yes of course I do darling, thank you. I seem to be in an odd mood today, getting old and nostalgic I suppose.'

'I don't know what there is to be nostalgic about. From what I've heard, life before the Awakening was like an apocalyptic nightmare.'

'What does apocalyptic mean?' asked Florence.

'It doesn't matter Florence, it means very bad, OK? Now come and play with your brother in the garden.'

'But I want to stay with 3G,' she whined.

'Go with your mother, my darling,' said Philip, 'and we can talk again later.'

'But...'

'No buts,' said her mother quickly. 'Come along with me young lady.'

They left Philip alone with his thoughts. Once he got into one of these downward mental spirals, it was hard to break free. He looked at the £20 note again and his eyes misted. *Bloody hell*, he muttered under his breath.

The sun was shining brightly and the air in the garden was warm. Since they'd discovered how to control the weather using an ionised particle ray, it only rained at night and the snow only fell on the hills and mountains, especially the ski resorts. Nobody noticed the weather much anymore because it was invariably pleasant. The children were playing on hoverboards, racing down the long lawn towards the orchard when Philip emerged from the house.

'Happy birthday, old chap,' said Joe, as he poured drinks for the gathered family. They sat around Philip's vintage, wooden trestle table, which he'd been given for his last birthday. Eight faces smiled in his direction and he managed to smile back, accepting a glass of organic wine.

'Cheers!' he said, and took a sip.

'Cheers!'

Philip noticed that his wife, Beverley, wasn't smiling. She'd sensed something about his manner that he couldn't hide from her, he was sure of it. After more than a hundred years of marriage, there was no concealing anything. They were almost one person really. He avoided her eyes and went towards the children.

'Is there something wrong with Philip today?' asked Joe.

'Just old age,' replied Beverley. She got up from the table and went after him. She caught up with him by the potting shed.

'Black dog at your heels again?'

He looked straight ahead and swallowed hard. 'I think it's time.'

'Time for what?'

Philip just looked into her eyes without saying a word and could tell immediately she understood.

'Nonsense, you're fit and strong. Besides, your family need you.'

'Do they? What for?'

Beverley hesitated. There was no easy answer to that. 'To share things with, to enjoy time with.'

'I've done that and more. I've run out of reasons.'

Philip's shoulders sagged. He hadn't felt this way since he'd turned 100. The great grandchildren had helped then, and the next generation too, especially Florence. Beverley knew this only too well.

'Florence needs you,' she said, looking away.

Philip forgave her the manipulation. 'What about what I need?'

'And what is that?'

'To know… to know what comes next and find out if I have a soul.'

'Religion is a thing of the past Philip, you know that. No religion, no faith. No faith, no soul. You'd better just enjoy what we have here and now.'

'I can't accept that Bev. Never have, never will.'

'That's dangerous talk. You could end up at the reconditioning lab.'

'That's exactly why I need to call it a day, darling. This so called utopia has stolen something precious, something I can't ever get back, not in this life.'

'There is only *this life,* can't you just pretend to accept that and wait until our appointed time?'

'Not anymore.'

Beverley put her arm around his waist. He could feel her trembling. Normally, this would be enough to make him weaken. Not this time.

'What will you do?' she asked.

'Today I will enjoy my birthday party. Tomorrow, I will go the Centre, download my knowledge early and offer myself up for research.'

'Things will look different in the morning,' she said.

He shook his head. 'I do hope not.'

'Look, 3G,' shouted Florence, 'one leg!'

The children whizzed by, shrieking with laughter.

The next morning, at 6am, a loud buzz from the front door startled them both.

'Who on earth…?' Philip rose from his breakfast to answer, still in his dressing gown and slippers. With a gesture of his hand the crystal glass door transformed from opaque to clear, revealing two men in white suits and sunglasses, regarding him dispassionately.

'Mr Watson?' asked one, 'Mr Philip Watson?'

'Yes, that's me.'

An identification badge was thrust towards his face.

'You've been selected for reconditioning, sir, please come with us.'

Philip recoiled in horror. 'No! This can't be... I'm a good citizen!'

And then it dawned on him. With growing realisation he turned to find Beverley. She was watching on from the kitchen, fresh tears streaking her face.

'I'm so sorry my darling,' she sobbed, 'but I couldn't bear to lose you.'

Philip didn't say another word. There was nothing more to say. He knew that within twenty-four hours he would be back in his favourite armchair and all this would be forgotten. But the look of betrayal on his face as their eyes met, he knew Beverley would remember that look until her dying day.

A Coat Tale

It was only a coat. And not even a great coat. By that I mean it wasn't all that good, rather than implying its style. But I loved it, and when I left it languishing on a train somewhere between Budapest and Catavecs, a small industrial town just over the Croatian border, I thought I'd never see it again.

Why was I on a train in Eastern Europe during the 1990s? For the purposes of this story, that doesn't really matter. This strange adventure truly began, when somewhere in the middle of the Hungarian countryside, the train juddered to a halt. I looked out of the grime-streaked window expecting to see another crumbling station, a few scruffy cigarette-smoking men or at least another bored-looking guard in a dusty old uniform. But there was nothing of the sort – just fields as far as the eye could see and little else.

The shabby compartment in which I sat contained only me. I got up, slid open the door and peered down the empty corridor. Apparently no one else was curious about our unscheduled stop, but I felt compelled to investigate anyway. As I wandered down the aisle, I glanced left and right for signs of activity but there were none. All the other compartments in my carriage were similarly empty, so when I reached the door through to the next carriage I resolved to continue on, with only a hint of increased urgency.

With growing anxiety, I realised the next carriage was also deserted. However, my momentary panic appeared premature when I suddenly discerned some movement in the distance. The window was too greasy to see much, but it was definitely a milling of people. I relaxed a little and kept going. It was when I was about three carriages away from my own that the clanking started. Clang! Clang!

Kachung! Screech! A brief respite then... Clang! Clunk! Screech again.

The train began to protest to this onslaught by shaking in tremulous waves and I found myself hanging on by pushing against the windows on either side of me. Then we were moving again, painfully slow at first, but then with greater ease and finally, with restored vigour. For a moment I considered proceeding to the more populated end of the train to see if I could find out what just happened. But then, remembering the frustrating conversation whilst buying a ticket earlier that day in the central station of Hungary's capital city, Budapest, I thought better of it and did an about turn.

I didn't get far. I returned to the other end of the carriage just in time to glimpse the remainder of the train, the back end... *my* end... disappearing into the distance. I'd been uncoupled... or rather my beloved coat had, along with my wallet, phone and my two remaining cheese sandwiches. I involuntarily shouted '*Stop!*' before realising how ridiculous that was. Reality dawned, quickly and painfully.

It had been my grandfather's coat, you see. The one he'd worn when we'd walked together in Scotland; from east to west across the Trossachs, over forty years ago. He loved to draw, and I remember photographing him in the coat, sketching, as we sat in a meadow with black flies buzzing around our heads. He was shorter than me and broader at that time. He was 70 and I was 17. The coat I captured in that picture would have hung loosely on my skinny seventeen-year-old frame, but now it seemed I was turning into him, and in more ways than I cared to admit. These days it fitted me like a glove and had become part of my history... my inheritance.

The wallet, phone and cheese sandwiches could all be

replaced… but the coat? The coat *was* my grandfather, or at least the precious memory of him. I could still see the panoramic view from the top of Ben Lomond, feel the gentle sway of the boat on Loch Katrine, and hear his rumbling voice, relating stories of his past as we lay in the quiet, soft gloom of the Youth Hostel dormitory. One halting, devastating tale still troubles me. That of his first baby son, lost to medical malpractice in the 1930s… George… George Watson. The one and only time I was to hear of him.

But love doesn't end because someone dies. I still love my grandfather and he still loved George, even though he'd only known him for a few weeks. There was no National Health Service in those days, and saving lives cost money. Granda worked as a painter in Wallsend upon Tyne's shipyards and didn't have very much money, not enough anyway. Should I tell you what happened to George? No, I don't think it's necessary. The story is woven into the fabric of that coat, one textured thread of many that draped around my shoulders, or at least used to.

Tears welled up in my eyes, frustration and anger flushed the cheeks of my otherwise ashen face. I even thought of jumping off the train and walking back along the line, but decided instead to get off at the next stop and try to make my situation known to… to whom exactly? Who on earth was I going to persuade that my old coat was so important? How could I even begin to explain what had happened? I hadn't met anyone outside of central Zagreb or Budapest who spoke more than three words of English. And what if the back-end of my train was at this moment hurtling off with a new engine, with a new purpose, in a new direction?

Mercifully, the next station wasn't far. Within about a quarter of an hour I was pushing my way through the swing door of what appeared to be a well-worn waiting room. An acrid cloud of cigarette smoke hung in the air, emanating from two unsavoury looking characters in blue overalls, playing cards in one corner. They didn't even look up. On the right, an old and crumpled lady nursed a basket of bruised fruit. On the left, a young, sallow-faced man sat texting on a very old and clunky looking mobile phone.

'Does anyone here speak English?' I asked, more in hope than expectation.

The card players continued without pause. The old lady became even more crumpled as she visibly tried to make herself smaller. The young man continued to text. I sighed and turned to leave.

'What is your problem?'

I stopped. It was the young man. He'd placed his phone on the table in front of him and regarded me now with dark, watery eyes. Now that I looked more closely I could see he was relatively well dressed and his dark hair slicked back with oil or gel. He could have been twenty or thirty, it was hard to tell.

'Well, this is going to sound ridiculous,' I began.

'Try me,' he said.

'OK... I was on that train that just left. About ten miles back it split, leaving me in one end and my belongings in the other. I need to get them back.'

The young man stared at me for a few seconds and then started to laugh. It began as a snort, then, bit by bit this evolved into a full-blown belly laugh. Almost breathless, he turned to relate the story to the room and soon they were all laughing, even the old woman was gleefully exposing a mouthful of glistening gums.

'I'm pleased to have cheered you all up!' I snapped, and stormed out.

I was standing on the edge of the platform, quietly seething when the young man came to my side.

'Hey, why don't you just forget about your stuff?' he said. 'Claim it off your insurance.'

'I can't,' I replied. 'It's irreplaceable.'

'What is?'

'My coat.'

'Your coat? This must be a very expensive coat, yes?'

'Not really. It belonged to my grandfather.'

'Oh… I see. In that case you had better come with me.'

I looked at him a little unsure, but something in his manner had changed. 'Come,' he urged me, walking towards the exit. Mutely, I followed.

We arrived at his car. The most battered, beaten-up Toyota I'd ever seen. It wasn't the type of car I would have expected him to drive at all. 'Where are we going?' I asked, looking at it dubiously.

'That half of the train will go to my village,' he replied. 'Get in.'

The passenger door creaked open to reveal what could only be described as the "remains" of the seat, but I did as he suggested and got in. The Toyota coughed, then spluttered but reluctantly started. It threatened to die more than once, but surprisingly, we were on the move.

'You were, erm, close to your grandfather?' he asked, in his thick but decipherable accent. His English was surprisingly good.

'Yes,' I replied.

'Me also,' he stated, staring straight ahead.

I simply nodded and with those few words we'd become sort of comrades, part of the same bizarre quest. This man had grown in my estimation.

'What's your name?' I asked.

'You would say Peter. Yours?'

'Philip,' I said with a smile, and we shook hands across the gearstick. 'You're the first person I've met in Hungary who speaks English well, Peter.'

'Thank you,' he replied, 'but we cannot expect the world to speak Hungarian.'

The village appeared as the Toyota rounded a long bend and finally died with an exhalation of steamy, greasy, oily breath. 'If I find my wallet I'll help you fix that,' I said, getting out.

'It does not matter,' he replied. 'It is not my car. Let us go now and get the coat of your grandfather.'

We walked the remaining few hundred metres to the village, turned right down a steep bank, crossed what appeared to be a rubbish dump, and ended up at a railway siding, where the offending train now sat inert, like some sort of monument.

'Where did you sit?' he asked, lighting up a cigarette

I pointed. 'Right at the back.' We walked towards the door at the rear of the train just as the guard was jumping out. He was wearing my grandfather's coat. I scowled, grinding my teeth. 'That's my coat he's wearing!'

The guard growled back, nudging me to one side whilst mumbling something I couldn't understand. A furious conversation broke out between this burly, unshaven guard and my new friend Peter, which escalated to pushing. This guy wasn't going to give up my coat without a fight.

'Stop!' I shouted, and remarkably they both did. 'Peter, please tell him he can keep my wallet. All I want is the coat.'

Peter looked disgusted but did as I asked. The guard must have told him where to get off, because Peter suddenly launched himself at the startled offender, throwing him onto his back. A sickening crunch filled the air and the guard lay still beneath Peter, who was now kneeling on his chest looking rather bewildered.

'Oh shit, Peter. Shit, shit, shit!' I hissed.

Peter got up and backed away silently, visibly shocked now. The guard remained immobile.

'Get your coat,' he said at last, flicking away his cigarette and regaining his composure.

'You're going to have to help me,' I replied, just about holding back my panic.

Together we managed to roll the guard over, revealing the bloody rock on which he had hit his head. I noticed that his grey hair was matted with blood. The coat, now removed, felt warm and strange in my hands.

'What do we do now?' I asked.

Peter kept his eyes on the guard. 'We dump him.'

Something in his casual manner unnerved me. I stared aghast as he lit another cigarette. 'I'm not the dumping of bodies type Peter. You can't be serious, we should seek help.'

Peter was unmoved. 'If you wish to see one of our Soviet-style jails, we get help. If you prefer to return home with your grandfather's coat, we dump him.'

I considered this for a few moments. 'Dump him where?' I asked.

'At the house of my uncle. He will know what to do. Take his feet.'

Reluctantly I obeyed and with Peter at the other end we trudged slowly up the hill, carrying our fate like a rolled up carpet. Amazingly, there was nobody around to see this tortuous journey, so we paused to get our breath back, and that's when a moment of clarity dawned.

'Peter, wait!'

We stopped and put down the load. 'There were no witnesses Peter, he could have just fallen from the train and banged his head. We could be just making things worse by taking the body to your uncle's house.'

'You are right,' replied Peter. 'We should take him back. We could place him as though he has fallen from the train.'

This was now playing out like a farce. We trudged back to the train, almost out of strength, the guard's backside dragging along in the dirt. And then, just as we arrived back where we started, the guard, inexplicably, began to stir. 'Ohhhhhh...' he moaned '...ahhhhhh.'

We dropped him like a hot potato and leaped back.

'Now what?' I asked.

'Well, we can choose,' replied Peter, calmly. 'Either we, how do you say it? Ah yes, either we face the tune or...'

'It's the music, not the tune.'

'Excuse me?'

'We say, face the music not face the tune.'

'Ah, thank you. So, we face the music or...'

'Or what?'

'Or we bang his head a little more.'

'Bang his... no, no way Peter, not likely, that's, that's murder. Don't even think about it.'

Peter shrugged. 'OK, then we face the music.' He took out his phone and started to punch in a number.

'Who... who are you calling?' I stammered.

'My uncle,' replied Peter, with a half-smile. 'I'm not a "facing the music" type. My uncle may have something on this vonatvédő that will make him... mmm... forget what happened today.'

'*Urrrggghhhhhh,*' went the guard, starting to come round.

'Your uncle sounds like he has influence,' I said, beginning to get the picture.

'Of a kind, yes,' replied Peter. But then someone must have answered his call because he began an unintelligible conversation that ebbed and flowed between what sounded like anger and pleading.

Abruptly the guard sat up, spitting what were probably obscenities. He put his hand to the back of his head, bringing back blood, before regaining his rather shaky legs, eyes now filled with hate. Peter ended his call and casually approached the guard. Violence seemed very close as the guard took hold of a baton which had been clipped to his belt. Peter, however, remained calm. He whispered three words at the guard and at once the anger in the guard's face turned to shock, then surprise and what may have just have been fear. He reached into his back pocket and brought out my wallet, throwing it in my direction, followed by the phone. I picked them up and returned them to *my* coat pockets. The guard backed away groggily, turned and stumbled away, cursing as he went.

'What the hell did you say to him?'

'You do not want to know. My uncle knows everything about everyone. It's probably time for you to continue with your journey now, Philip. The next train is in one hour.'

'How can I ever repay you?' I asked.

Peter laughed. 'You have a new story pressed into the, er, weaving of your grandfather's coat now. Each time you fasten it, remember this day and smile.'

I smoothed my hands down the fabric of the coat, appreciating it again, remembering. 'An hour you say?'

Peter wobbled his head from side to side. 'Yes, or maybe a little more. This is Hungary after all.'

I nodded my understanding. 'Then tell me about *your* Grandfather,' I said.

'Ah, for that story the train is tomorrow… or maybe the day after that,' he replied.

I smiled. 'The day after tomorrow? Then we had better find a more comfortable place to sit.'

About the author

Philip M Stuckey is an award winning entrepreneur, singer-songwriter, author and poet, based in rural Northumberland. His writing often leans towards esoteric themes, asking questions about the nature of existence through the experiences of his characters. His songs evoke a strong sense of place and his stories are immersed in empathy.

Some of the critically-acclaimed songs are expressions of the stories included in the *Matters of Life and Death* collection and also within his forthcoming fantasy novel, *The Hunt for Moss and Magic*.

Music by Stuckfish

Calling

Calling is a combination of storytelling lyrics and fascinating, multi-layered musical journeys of the unexpected, with soaring guitars and dramatic vocal harmonies.

The Watcher

In *The Watcher*, the grand fantasy of a true magical family line, hunted to near extinction by the dark forces of chaos continues.

"'Fantastic melodic prog rock" (*Classic Rock Magazine*)

"It's little wonder the plaudits are coming in thick and fast for Stuckfish" (*Prog Rock Magazine*)

To order, visit the official Stuckfish website:
https://www.stuckfish.net/music

Other Publications by Bridge House

Days Pass like a Shadow

by Paula R.C. Readman

Within the pages of *Days Pass like a Shadow* are thirteen dark tales covering the theme of death and loss. At the centre of every story is a beating heart. For the reader to make the journey to that centre, along the flowing veins of the words, all they need is a few minutes during a lunch break, or at the end of the day. The reader will be introduced to a rich and diverse collection of characters - a gardener, a serial killer, a time traveller, a sleepwalker and many more..

Order from Amazon:

Paperback: ISBN 978-1-907335-80-8
eBook: ISBN 978-1-907335-81-5

Last Chance Salon

by *FJ McNeill*

"Who was I kidding? I wasn't a successful businessman running an empire from a luxury penthouse. I was a chain-smoking, fifty-something, sometime actor in a cardigan, washed-up in a stagnant corner of south London."

When Rafe Bunce takes over a run-down hair salon in Penge, he hopes to make a success of his life at last. Not content with improving his own fortunes, he is soon meddling in his customers' lives, too – with bittersweet results.

The stories in *Last Chance Salon* touch on the hopes and dreams, big and small, which we all carry inside us.

Order from Amazon:

Paperback: ISBN 978-1-907335-78-5
eBook: ISBN 978-1-907335-79-2

The Power of Love

by Phyllis J. Burton

The stories in *THE POWER OF LOVE* are quite simply about LOVE of all kinds. If you like romance, then these short stories are written just for you as well. There is plenty of that! The huge clock on Waterloo station acts as catalyst for that. But the collection also shows us other sorts of love: family ties, enduring love, old love, forbidden love, mended love, children's love for their parents, parents' love for their children, a love for old buildings, and love between animals and humans.

"If you're looking for short stories to read then look no further. These are great reads from Phyllis. The stories are tender, loving and well-written. I'd recommend these stories to everyone." (*Amazon*)

Order from Amazon:

Paperback: ISBN 978-1-907335-72-3
eBook: ISBN 978-1-907335-73-0